W.B. YEATS
Selected Poetry

COLLECTABLE CLASSICS
Special Gift Edition

FLAME TREE PUBLISHING
6 Melbray Mews, Fulham,
London SW6 3NS, United Kingdom
www.flametreepublishing.com

First published and copyright © 2021
Flame Tree Publishing Ltd

The poems in this selection derive from these original publications:
The Dublin University Review, pub. William McGee (May, 1885); *The Wind Among the Reeds*, pub. Elkin Matthews (London, 1899); *In the Seven Woods*, pub. The Dun Emer Press (Dundrum, Dublin, 1903); *Collected Works Vols I & II*, pub. A.H. Bullen (Shakespeare Head Press, Stratford-on-Avon, 1908); *The Green Helmet & Other Poems*, pub. Cuala Press (Dublin, 1910); *Poems Written in Discouragement*, pub. Cuala Press (Dublin, 1912–13); *Responsibilities: Poems and a Play*, pub. Cuala Press (Dublin, 1914); *The Wild Swans at Coole, Other Verses and a Play*, pub. Cuala Press (Dublin, 1917); the 1920 edition of *Poems* (1895) published by T. Fisher Unwin Ltd.; *Michael Robartes and the Dancer*, pub. Cuala Press (Dublin, 1921); *Seven Poems and a Fragment*, pub. Cuala Press (Dublin, 1922), *The Cat and the Moon and Certain Poems*, pub. Cuala Press (Dublin, 1924).

21 23 25 24 22
1 3 5 7 9 10 8 6 4 2

ISBN: 978-1-83964-219-7

Cover, pattern art and icons were created by Flame Tree Studio. Front cover photo is based on the 1903 photo of W.B. Yeats by Alice Boughton (1866–1943). The back cover is based on an image courtesy of Artdock/Shutterstock.

Judith John (Glossary) is a writer and editor specializing in literature and history. A former secondary school English Language and Literature teacher, she has subsequently worked as an editor on major educational projects, including *English A: Literature* for the Pearson International Baccalaureate series. Judith's major research interests include Romantic and Gothic literature, and Renaissance drama.

A copy of the CIP data for this book is available from the British Library.

Designed and created in the UK | Printed and bound in China

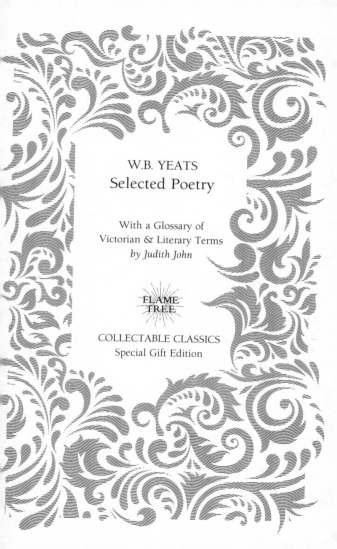

W.B. YEATS
Selected Poetry

With a Glossary of
Victorian & Literary Terms
by Judith John

FLAME
TREE

COLLECTABLE CLASSICS
Special Gift Edition

CONTENTS

W.B. YEATS
Selected Poetry

DREAMS, VISIONS
& ART ITSELF
⋅✳⋅

TO SOME I HAVE TALKED
WITH BY THE FIRE
(An introductory poem)

While I wrought out these fitful Danaan rhymes,
My heart would brim with dreams about the times
When we bent down above the fading coals;
And talked of the dark folk, who live in souls
Of passionate men, like bats in the dead trees;
And of the wayward twilight companies,
Who sigh with mingled sorrow and content,
Because their blossoming dreams have never bent
Under the fruit of evil and of good:
And of the embattled flaming multitude
Who rise, wing above wing, flame above flame,
And, like a storm, cry the Ineffable Name,
And with the clashing of their sword blades make
A rapturous music, till the morning break,
And the white hush end all, but the loud beat
Of their long wings, the flash of their white feet.

THE SONG OF
THE HAPPY SHEPHERD

The woods of Arcady are dead,
And over is their antique joy;
Of old the world on dreaming fed;
Gray Truth is now her painted toy;
Yet still she turns her restless head:
But O, sick children of the world,
Of all the many changing things
In dreary dancing past us whirled,
To the cracked tune that Chronos sings,
Words alone are certain good.
Where are now the warring kings,
Word be-mockers? – By the Rood
Where are now the warring kings?
An idle word is now their glory,
By the stammering schoolboy said,
Reading some entangled story:
The kings of the old time are fled
The wandering earth herself may be
Only a sudden flaming word,
In clanging space a moment heard,
Troubling the endless reverie.

Then nowise worship dusty deeds,
Nor seek; for this is also sooth;
To hunger fiercely after truth,

Lest all thy toiling only breeds
New dreams, new dreams; there is no truth
Saving in thine own heart. Seek, then,
No learning from the starry men,
Who follow with the optic glass
The whirling ways of stars that pass –
Seek, then, for this is also sooth,
No word of theirs – the cold star-bane
Has cloven and rent their hearts in twain,
And dead is all their human truth.
Go gather by the humming-sea
Some twisted, echo-harbouring shell,
And to its lips thy story tell,
And they thy comforters will be,
Rewarding in melodious guile,
Thy fretful words a little while,
Till they shall singing fade in ruth,
And die a pearly brotherhood;
For words alone are certain good:
Sing, then, for this is also sooth.

I must be gone: there is a grave
Where daffodil and lily wave,
And I would please the hapless faun,
Buried under the sleepy ground,
With mirthful songs before the dawn.
His shouting days with mirth were crowned;
And still I dream he treads the lawn,

Walking ghostly in the dew,
Pierced by my glad singing through,
My songs of old earth's dreamy youth:
But ah! she dreams not now; dream thou!
For fair are poppies on the brow:
Dream, dream, for this is also sooth.

THE SAD SHEPHERD

There was a man whom Sorrow named his friend,
And he, of his high comrade Sorrow dreaming,
Went walking with slow steps along the gleaming
And humming sands, where windy surges wend:
And he called loudly to the stars to bend
From their pale thrones and comfort him, but they
Among themselves laugh on and sing alway:
And then the man whom Sorrow named his friend
Cried out, *Dim sea, hear my most piteous story!*
The sea swept on and cried her old cry still,
Rolling along in dreams from hill to hill;
He fled the persecution of her glory
And, in a far-off, gentle valley stopping,
Cried all his story to the dewdrops glistening,
But naught they heard, for they are always listening,
The dewdrops, for the sound of their own dropping.
And then the man whom Sorrow named his friend,
Sought once again the shore, and found a shell,
And thought, *I will my heavy story tell*
Till my own words, re-echoing, shall send
Their sadness through a hollow, pearly heart;
And my own tale again for me shall sing,
And my own whispering words be comforting,
And lo! my ancient burden may depart.
Then he sang softly nigh the pearly rim;
But the sad dweller by the sea-ways lone
Changed all he sang to inarticulate moan
Among her wildering whirls, forgetting him.

THE CLOAK, THE BOAT, AND THE SHOES

"What do you make so fair and bright?"

"I make the cloak of Sorrow:
"O, lovely to see in all men's sight
"Shall be the cloak of Sorrow,
"In all men's sight."

"What do you build with sails for flight?"

"I build a boat for Sorrow,
"O, swift on the seas all day and night
"Saileth the rover Sorrow,
"All day and night."

"What do you weave with wool so white?

"I weave the shoes of Sorrow,
"Soundless shall be the footfall light
"In all men's ears of Sorrow,
"Sudden and light."

MICHAEL ROBARTES REMEMBERS FORGOTTEN BEAUTY

When my arms wrap you round I press
My heart upon the loveliness
That has long faded from the world;
The jewelled crowns that kings have hurled
In shadowy pools, when armies fled;
The love-tales wave with silken thread
By dreaming ladies upon cloth
That has made fat the murderous moth;
The roses that of old time were
Woven by ladies in their hair,
The dew-cold lilies ladies bore
Through many a sacred corridor
Where such gray clouds of incense rose
That only the gods' eyes did not close:
For that pale breast and lingering hand
Come from a more dream-heavy land,
A more dream-heavy hour than this;
And when you sigh from kiss to kiss
I hear white Beauty sighing, too,
For hours when all must fade like dew
But flame on flame, deep under deep,
Throne over throne, where in half sleep
Their swords upon their iron knees
Brood her high lonely mysteries.

TO MY HEART, BIDDING IT HAVE NO FEAR

Be you still, be you still, trembling heart;
Remember the wisdom out of the old days:
Him who trembles before the flame and the flood,
And the winds that blow through the starry ways,
Let the starry winds and the flame and the flood
Cover over and hide, for he has no part
With the proud, majestical multitude.

THE CAP AND BELLS

The jester walked in the garden:
The garden had fallen still;
He bade his soul rise upward
And stand on her window-sill.

It rose in a straight blue garment,
When owls began to call:
It had grown wise-tongued by thinking
Of a quiet and light footfall;

But the young queen would not listen;
She rose in her pale night gown;
She drew in the heavy casement
And pushed the latches down.

He bade his heart go to her,
When the owls called out no more;
In a red and quivering garment
It sang to her through the door.

It had grown sweet-tongued by dreaming,
Of a flutter of flower-like hair;
But she took up her fan from the table
And waved it off on the air.

"I have cap and bells" he pondered,
"I will send them to her and die;"
And when the morning whitened
He left them where she went by.

She laid them upon her bosom,
Under a cloud of her hair,
And her red lips sang them a love song:
Till stars grew out of the air.

She opened her door and her window,
And the heart and the soul came through,
To her right hand came the red one,
To her left hand came the blue,

They set up a noise like crickets,
A chattering wise and sweet,
And her hair was a folded flower
And the quiet of love in her feet.

THE VALLEY OF THE BLACK PIG

The dews drop slowly and dreams gather:
   unknown spears
Suddenly hurtle before my dream-awakened eyes,
And then the clash of fallen horsemen and the cries
Of unknown perishing armies beat about my ears.
We who still labour by the cromlec on the shore,
The grey cairn on the hill, when day sinks drowned
   in dew,
Being weary of the world's empires, bow down to you
Master of the still stars and of the flaming door.

MICHAEL ROBARTES ASKS FORGIVENESS BECAUSE OF HIS MANY MOODS

If this importunate heart trouble your peace
With words lighter than air,
Or hopes that in mere hoping flicker and cease;
Crumple the rose in your hair;
And cover your lips with odorous twilight and say,
"O Hearts of wind-blown flame!
"O Winds, elder than changing of night and wday,
"That murmuring and longing came,
"From marble cities loud with tabors of old
"In dove-gray faery lands;
"From battle banners fold upon purple fold,
"Queens wrought with glimmering hands;
"That saw young Niamh hover with love-lorn face
"Above the wandering tide;
"And lingered in the hidden desolate place,
"Where the last Phoenix died
"And wrapped the flames above his holy head;
"And still murmur and long:
"O Piteous Hearts, changing till change be dead
"In a tumultuous song:"
And cover the pale blossoms of your breast
With your dim heavy hair,
And trouble with a sigh for all things longing for rest.
The odorous twilight there.

AEDH TELLS OF A VALLEY FULL OF LOVERS

I dreamed that I stood in a valley, and amid sighs,
For happy lovers passed two by two where I stood;
And I dreamed my lost love came stealthily out of
    the wood
With her cloud-pale eyelids falling on dream-
    dimmed eyes:
I cried in my dream *"O women bid the young men lay*
"Their heads on your knees, and drown their eyes
    with your hair,
"Or remembering hers they will find no other
    face fair
"Till all the valleys of the world have been
    withered away."

AEDH TELLS OF THE PERFECT BEAUTY

O cloud-pale eyelids, dream-dimmed eyes
The poets labouring all their days
To build a perfect beauty in rhyme
Are overthrown by a woman's gaze
And by the unlabouring brood of the skies:
And therefore my heart will bow, when dew
Is dropping sleep, until God burn time,
Before the unlabouring stars and you.

AEDH HEARS THE CRY OF THE SEDGE

I wander by the edge
Of this desolate lake
Where wind cries in the sedge
Until the axle break
That keeps, the stars in their round
And hands hurl in the deep
The banners of East and West
And the girdle of light is unbound,
Your head will not lie on the breast
Of your beloved in sleep.

AEDH THINKS OF THOSE WHO HAVE
SPOKEN EVIL OF HIS BELOVED

Half close your eyelids, loosen your hair,
And dream about the great and their pride;
They have spoken against you everywhere,
But weigh this song with the great and their pride;
I made it out of a mouthful of air,
Their children's children shall say they have lied.

HANRAHAN LAMENTS BECAUSE OF HIS WANDERINGS

O where is our Mother of Peace
Nodding her purple hood?
For the winds that awakened the stars
Are blowing through my blood.
I would that the death-pale deer
Had come through the mountain side,
And trampled the mountain away,
And drunk up the murmuring tide;
For the winds that awakened the stars
Are blowing through my blood,
And our Mother of Peace has forgot me
Under her purple hood.

HANRAHAN SPEAKS TO THE LOVERS OF HIS SONGS IN COMING DAYS

O, colleens, kneeling by your altar rails long hence,
When songs I wove for my beloved hide the prayer,
And smoke from this dead heart drifts through the
    violet air
And covers away the smoke of myrrh
    and frankincense;
Bend down and pray for the great sin I wove in song,
Till Maurya of the wounded heart cry a sweet cry,
And call to my beloved and me: "No longer fly
"Amid the hovering, piteous, penitential throng."

THE WITHERING OF THE BOUGHS

I cried when the moon was murmuring to the birds
"Let peewit call and curlew cry where they will
I long for your merry and tender and pitiful words,
For the roads are unending and there is no place to
    my mind."
The honey-pale moon lay low on the sleepy hill
And I fell asleep upon lonely Echtge of streams;
No boughs have withered because of the wintry wind,
The boughs have withered because I have told them
    my dreams.

I know of the leafy paths that the witches take,
Who come with their crowns of pearl and their
    spindles of wool,
And their secret smile, out of the depths of the lake;
And of apple islands where the Danaan kind
Wind and unwind their dances when the light
    grows cool
On the island lawns, their feet where the pale
    foam gleams;
No boughs have withered because of the wintry wind,
The boughs have withered because I have told them
    my dreams.

I know of the sleepy country, where swans fly round
Coupled with golden chains and sing as they fly,

A king and a queen are wandering there, and
   the sound
Has made them so happy and hopeless, so deaf and
   so blind
With wisdom, they wander till all the years have
   gone by;
I know, and the curlew and peewit on Echtge
   of streams;
No boughs have withered because of the wintry wind,
The boughs have withered because I have told them
   my dreams.

ADAM'S CURSE

We sat together at one summer's end
That beautiful mild woman your close friend
And you and I, and talked of poetry.

I said "a line will take us hours maybe,
Yet if it does not seem a moment's thought
Our stitching and unstitching has been naught.
Better go down upon your marrow bones
And scrub a kitchen pavement, or break stones
Like an old pauper in all kinds of weather;
For to articulate sweet sounds together
Is to work harder than all these and yet
Be thought an idler by the noisy set
Of bankers, schoolmasters, and clergymen
The martyrs call the world."

                              That woman then
Murmured with her young voice, for whose mild sake
There's many a one shall find out all heartache
In finding that it's young and mild and low.
"There is one thing that all we women know
Although we never heard of it at school,
That we must labour to be beautiful."

I said, "It's certain there is no fine thing
Since Adam's fall but needs much labouring.

There have been lovers who thought love should be
So much compounded of high courtesy
That they would sigh and quote with learned looks
Precedents out of beautiful old books;
Yet now it seems an idle trade enough".

We sat grown quiet at the name of love.
We saw the last embers of daylight die
And in the trembling blue-green of the sky
A moon, worn as if it had been a shell
Washed by time's waters as they rose and fell
About the stars and broke in days and years.

I had a thought for no one's but your ears;
That you were beautiful and that I strove
To love you in the old high way of love;
That it had all seemed happy, and yet we'd grown
As weary hearted as that hollow moon.

UNDER THE MOON

I have no happiness in dreaming of Brycelinde;
Nor Avalon the grass green hollow, nor Joyous Isle,
Where one found Lancelot crazed and hid him for
   a while,
Nor Ulad when Naoise had thrown a sail upon
   the wind,
Nor lands that seem too dim to be burdens on
   the heart,
Land-under-Wave, where out of the moon's light and
   the sun's
Seven old sisters wind the threads of the long
   lived ones,
Land-of-the-Tower, where Aengus has thrown the
   gates apart,
And Wood-of-Wonders, where one kills an ox at dawn
To find it when night falls laid on a golden bier:
Therein are many queens like Branwen,
   and Guinivere;
And Niamh, and Laban, and Fand, who could change
   to an otter or fawn
And the wood-woman whose lover was changed to a
   blue-eyed hawk;
And whether I go in my dreams by woodland, or dun,
   or shore,
Or on the unpeopled waves with kings to pull at
   the oar,

I hear the harpstring praise them or hear their
    mournful talk.
Because of a story I heard under the thin horn
Of the third moon, that hung between the night and
    the day,
To dream of women whose beauty was folded
    in dismay,
Even in an old story, is a burden not to be borne.

THE PLAYERS ASK FOR A BLESSING ON THE PSALTERIES AND THEMSELVES

THREE VOICES TOGETHER
Hurry to bless the hands that play
The mouths that speak, the notes and strings
O masters of the glittering town!
O! lay the shrilly trumpet down,
Though drunken with the flags that sway
Over the ramparts and the towers,
And with the waving of your wings.

FIRST VOICE
Maybe they linger by the way;
One gathers up his purple gown;
One leans and mutters by the wall;
He dreads the weight of mortal hours.

SECOND VOICE
O no, O no, they hurry down
Like plovers that have heard the call.

THIRD VOICE
O, kinsmen of the Three in One,
O, kinsmen bless the hands that play.
The notes they waken shall live on
When all this heavy history's done.
Our hands, our hands must ebb away.

THREE VOICES TOGETHER
The proud and careless notes live on
But bless our hands that ebb away.

THE RIDER FROM THE NORTH
From the play of The Country of the Young

There's many a strong farmer
Who's heart would break in two
If he could see the townland
That we are riding to;
Boughs have their fruit and blossom,
At all times of the year,
Rivers are running over
With red beer and brown beer.
An old man plays the bagpipes
In a golden and silver wood,
Queens their eyes blue like the ice
Are dancing in a crowd.

The little fox he murmured,
O what is the world's bane?,
The sun was laughing sweetly,
The moon plucked at my rein;
But the little red fox murmured
"O do not pluck at his rein,
He is riding to the townland
That is the world's bane."

When their hearts are so high,
That they would come to blows,
They unhook their heavy swords

From golden and silver boughs;
But all that are killed in battle
Awaken to life again;
It is lucky that their story
Is not known among men.
For O the strong farmers
That would let the spade lie,
For their hearts would be like a cup
That somebody had drunk dry.

The little fox he murmured,
"O what is the world's bane?"
The sun was laughing sweetly,
The moon plucked at my rein;
But the little red fox murmured
"O do not pluck at his rein,
He is riding to the townland
That is the world's bane."

Michael will unhook his trumpet
From a bough overhead,
And blow a little noise
When the supper has been spread.
Gabriel will come from the water
With a fish tail, and talk
Of wonders that have happened
On wet roads where men walk,
And lift up an old horn

Of hammered silver, and drink
Till he has fallen asleep
Upon the starry brink.

The little fox he murmured,
"O what is the world's bane,?"
The sun was laughing sweetly,
The moon plucked at my rein;
But the little red fox murmured,
"O do not pluck at his rein,
He is riding to the townland,
That is the world's bane."

HIS DREAM

I swayed upon the gaudy stern
The butt end of a steering oar.
And everywhere that I could turn
Men ran upon the shore.

And though I would have hushed the crowd
There was no mother's son, but said,
"What is the figure in a shroud
Upon a gaudy bed?"

And fishes bubbling to the brim
Cried out upon that thing beneath.
It had such dignity of limb,
By the sweet name of Death"

Though I'd my finger on my lip.
What could I but take up the song?
And fish and crowd and gaudy ship
Cried out the whole night long.

Crying amid the glittering sea.
Naming it with ecstatic breath.
Because it had such dignity
By the sweet name of Death.

THE CONSOLATION

I had this thought awhile ago.
My darling cannot understand
What I have done, or what would do
In this blind bitter land;

And I grew weary of the sun
Until my thoughts cleared up again.
Remembering that the best I have done
Was done to make it plain;

That every year I have cried at length
My darling understands it all.
Because I have come into my strength.
And words obey my call;

That had she done so who can say
What would have shaken from the sieve?
I might have thrown poor words away
And been content to live.

THE FASCINATION OF WHAT'S DIFFICULT

The fascination of what's difficult
Has dried the sap out of my veins, and rent
Spontaneous joy and natural content
Out of my heart. There's something ails our colt
That must, as if it had not holy blood,
Nor on an Olympus leaped from cloud to cloud,
Shiver under the lash, strain, sweat, and jolt
As though it dragged road metal. My curse on plays
That have to be set up in fifty ways,
On the day's war with every knave and dolt,
Theatre business, management of men.
I swear before the dawn comes round again
I'll find the stable and pull out the bolt.

TO A POET, WHO WOULD HAVE ME PRAISE CERTAIN BAD POETS, IMITATORS OF HIS AND OF MINE

You say as I have often given tongue
In praise of what another's said or sung
'Twere politic to do the like by these,
But where's the wild dog that has praised his fleas?

ALL THINGS CAN TEMPT ME

All things can tempt me from this craft of verse,
One time it was a woman's face, or worse
The seeming needs of my fool-driven land;
Now nothing but comes readier to the hand
Than this accustomed toil. When I was young,
I had not given a penny for a song
Did not the poet sing it with such airs,
That one believed he had a sword upstairs,
Yet would be now, could I but have my wish,
Colder and dumber and deafer than a fish.

INTRODUCTORY RHYMES

Pardon, old fathers, if you still remain
Somewhere in ear-shot for the story's end,
Old Dublin merchant 'free of ten and four'
Or trading out of Galway into Spain;
And country scholar, Robert Emmet's friend,
A hundred-year-old memory to the poor;
Traders or soldiers who have left me blood
That has not passed through any huxter's loin,
Pardon, and you that did not weigh the cost,
Old Butlers when you took to horse and stood
Beside the brackish waters of the Boyne
Till your bad master blenched and all was lost;
And merchant skipper that leaped overboard
After a ragged hat in Biscay Bay,
You most of all, silent and fierce old man
Because you were the spectacle that stirred
My fancy, and set my boyish lips to say
"Only the wasteful virtues earn the sun";
Pardon that for a barren passion's sake,
Although I have come close on forty-nine
I have no child, I have nothing but a book,
Nothing but that to prove your blood and mine.

THE REALISTS

Hope that you may understand!
What can books of men that wive
In a dragon-guarded land,
Paintings of the dolphin-drawn
Sea-nymphs in their pearly waggons
Do, but awake a hope to live
That had gone
With the dragons?

I: THE WITCH

Toil and grow rich,
What's that but to lie
With a foul witch
And after, drained dry,
To be brought
To the chamber where
Lies one long sought
With despair.

II: THE PEACOCK

What's riches to him
That has made a great peacock
With the pride of his eye?
The wind-beaten, stone-grey,
And desolate Three-rock
Would nourish his whim.
Live he or die
Amid wet rocks and heather,
His ghost will be gay
Adding feather to feather
For the pride of his eye.

THE DOLLS

A doll in the doll-maker's house
Looks at the cradle and balls:
"That is an insult to us."
But the oldest of all the dolls
Who had seen, being kept for show,
Generations of his sort,
Out-screams the whole shelf: "Although
There's not a man can report
Evil of this place,
The man and the woman bring
Hither to our disgrace,
A noisy and filthy thing."
Hearing him groan and stretch
The doll-maker's wife is aware
Her husband has heard the wretch,
And crouched by the arm of his chair,
She murmurs into his ear,
Head upon shoulder leant:
"My dear, my dear, oh dear,
It was an accident."

A COAT

I made my song a coat
Covered with embroideries
Out of old mythologies
From heel to throat;
But the fools caught it,
Wore it in the world's eye
As though they'd wrought it.
Song, let them take it
For there's more enterprise
In walking naked.

CLOSING RHYMES

While I, from that reed-throated whisperer
Who comes at need, although not now as once
A clear articulation in the air
But inwardly, surmise companions
Beyond the fling of the dull ass's hoof,
– Ben Jonson's phrase – and find when June is come
At Kyle-na-no under that ancient roof
A sterner conscience and a friendlier home
I can forgive even that wrong of wrongs.
Those undreamt accidents that have made me
– Seeing that Fame has perished this long while
Being but a part of ancient ceremony –
Notorious, till all my priceless things
Are but a post the passing dogs defile.

LINES WRITTEN IN DEJECTION

When have I last looked on
The round green eyes and the long wavering bodies
Of the dark leopards of the moon?
All the wild witches those most noble ladies,
For all their broom-sticks and their tears,
Their angry tears, are gone.
The holy centaurs of the hills are banished;
And I have nothing but harsh sun;
Heroic mother moon has vanished,
And now that I have come to fifty years
I must endure the timid sun.

THE DAWN

I would be as ignorant as the dawn
That has looked down
On that old queen measuring a town
With the pin of a brooch,
Or on the withered men that saw
From their pedantic Babylon
The careless planets in their courses,
The stars fade out where the moon comes,
And took their tablets and did sums;
I would be as ignorant as the dawn
That merely stood, rocking the glittering coach
Above the cloudy shoulders of the horses;
I would be – for no knowledge is worth a straw –
Ignorant and wanton as the dawn.

THE FISHERMAN

Although I can see him still
The freckled man who goes
To a gray place on a hill
In gray Connemara clothes
At dawn to cast his flies;
It's long since I began
To call up to the eyes
This wise and simple man.
All day I'd looked in the face
What I had hoped 'twould be
To write for my own race
And the reality;
The living men that I hate
The dead man that I loved,
The craven man in his seat,
The insolent unreproved
And no knave brought to book
Who has won a drunken cheer,
The witty man and his joke
Aimed at the commonest ear,
The clever man who cries
The catch-cries of the clown,
The beating down of the wise
And great Art beaten down.

May be a twelvemonth since
Suddenly I began,
In scorn of this audience
Imagining a man,
And his sun-freckled face,
And gray Connemara cloth,
Climbing up to a place
Where stone is dark with froth,
And the down turn of his wrist
When the flies drop in the stream;
A man who does not exist
A man who is but a dream;
And cried "before I am old
I shall have written him one
Poem may be as cold
And passionate as the dawn."

THE HAWK

Call down the hawk from the air;
Let him be hooded or caged
Till the yellow eye has grown mild,
For larder and spit are bare,
The old cook enraged,
The scullion gone wild.

"I will not be clapped in a hood,
Nor a cage, nor alight upon wrist,
Now I have learnt to be proud
Hovering over the wood
In the broken mist
Or tumbling cloud."

What tumbling cloud did you cleave,
Yellow-eyed hawk of the mind,
Last evening? that I, who had sat
Dumbfounded before a knave,
Should give to my friend
A pretence of wit.

PRESENCES

This night has been so strange that it seemed
As if the hair stood up on my head.
From going-down of the sun I have dreamed
That women laughing, or timid or wild,
In rustle of lace or silken stuff,
Climbed up my creaking stair. They had read
All I had rhymed of that monstrous thing
Returned and yet unrequited love.
They stood in the door and stood between
My great wood lecturn and the fire
Till I could hear their hearts beating:
One is a harlot, and one a child
That never looked upon man with desire,
And one it may be a queen.

THE BALLOON OF THE MIND

Hands do what you're bid;
Bring the balloon of the mind
That bellies and drags in the wind
Into its narrow shed.

EGO DOMINUS TUUS

HIC

On the grey sand beside the shallow stream
Under your old wind-beaten tower, where still
A lamp burns on beside the open book
That Michael Robartes left, you walk in the moon
And though you have passed the best of life still trace
Enthralled by the unconquerable delusion
Magical shapes.

ILLE

                     By the help of an image
I call to my own opposite, summon all
That I have handled least, least looked upon.

HIC

And I would find myself and not an image.

ILLE

That is our modern hope and by its light
We have lit upon the gentle, sensitive mind
And lost the old nonchalance of the hand;
Whether we have chosen chisel, pen or brush
We are but critics, or but half create
Timid, entangled, empty and abashed
Lacking the countenance of our friends.

HIC
                    And yet
The chief imagination of Christendom
Dante Alighieri so utterly found himself
That he has made that hollow face of his
More plain to the mind's eye than any face
But that of Christ.

ILLE
                    And did he find himself
Or was the hunger that had made it hollow
A hunger for the apple on the bough
Most out of reach? and is that spectral image
The man that Lapo and that Guido knew?
I think he fashioned from his opposite
An image that might have been a stony face,
Staring upon a bedouin's horse-hair roof
From doored and windowed cliff, or half upturned
Among the coarse grass and the camel dung.
He set his chisel to the hardest stone.
Being mocked by Guido for his lecherous life
Derided and deriding, driven out
To climb that stair and eat that bitter bread,
He found the unpersuadable justice, he found
The most exalted lady loved by a man.

HIC

Yet surely there are men who have made their art
Out of no tragic war, lovers of life.
Impulsive men that look for happiness
And sing when they have found it.

ILLE

                    No not sing
For those that love the world serve it in action,
Grow rich, popular and full of influence.
And should they paint or write still it is action:
The struggle of the fly in marmalade.
The rhetorician would deceive his neighbours
The sentimentalist himself; while art
Is but a vision of reality.
What portion in the world can the artist have
Who has awakened from the common dream
But dissipation and despair?

HIC

                    And yet
No one denies to Keats love of the world;
Remember his deliberate happiness.

ILLE

His art is happy but who knows his mind?
I see a school boy when I think of him
With face and nose pressed to a sweet-shop window,

For certainly he sank into his grave
His senses and his heart unsatisfied,
And made – being poor, ailing and ignorant,
Shut out from all the luxury of the world,
The ill-bred son of a livery stable-keeper –
Luxuriant song.

HIC

                    Why should you leave the lamp
Burning alone beside an open book.
And trace these characters upon the sands;
A style is found by sedentary toil
And by the imitation of great masters.

ILLE
Because I seek an image not a book.
Those men that in their writings are most wise
Own nothing but their blind, stupefied hearts.
I call to the mysterious one who yet
Shall walk the wet sands by the edge of the stream
And look most like me, being indeed my double,
And prove of all imaginable things
The most unlike, being my anti-self,
And standing by these characters disclose
All that I seek; and whisper it as though
He were afraid the birds, who cry aloud
Their momentary cries before it is dawn,
Would carry it away to blasphemous men.

AN IMAGE FROM A PAST LIFE

HE

Never until this night have I been stirred.
The elaborate star-light has thrown reflections
On the dark stream,
Till all the eddies gleam;
And thereupon there comes that scream
From terrified, invisible beast or bird:
Image of poignant recollection.

SHE

An image of my heart that is smitten through
Out of all likelihood, or reason,
And when at last,
Youth's bitterness being past,
I had thought that all my days were cast
Amid most lovely places; smitten as though
It had not learned its lesson.

HE

Why have you laid your hands upon my eyes?
What can have suddenly alarmed you
Whereon 'twere best
My eyes should never rest?
What is there but the slowly fading west,
The river imaging the flashing skies,
All that to this moment charmed you?

SHE
A sweetheart from another life floats there
As though she had been forced to linger
From vague distress
Or arrogant loveliness,
Merely to loosen out a tress
Among the starry eddies of her hair
Upon the paleness of a finger.

HE
But why should you grow suddenly afraid
And start – I at your shoulder –
Imagining
That any night could bring
An image up, or anything
Even to eyes that beauty had driven mad,
But images to make me fonder.

SHE
Now she has thrown her arms above her head;
Whether she threw them up to flout me,
Or but to find,
Now that no fingers bind,
That her hair streams upon the wind,
I do not know, that know I am afraid
Of the hovering thing night brought me.

SUGGESTED BY A PICTURE OF A
BLACK CENTAUR

Your hooves have stamped at the black margin of
    the wood,
Even where the horrible green parrots call and swing.
My works are all stamped down into the sultry mud.
I knew that horse play, knew it for a murderous thing.
What wholesome sun has ripened is wholesome food
    to eat
And that alone, yet I being driven half insane
Because of some green wing, gathered old
    mummy wheat
In the mad abstract dark and ground it grain by grain
And after baked it slowly in an oven; but now
I bring full flavoured wine out of a barrel found
Where seven Ephesian topers slept and never knew
When Alexander's empire past, they slept so sound.
Stretch out your limbs and sleep a long
    Saturnian sleep;
I have loved you better than my soul for all my words,
And there is none so fit to keep a watch and keep
Unwearied eyes upon those horrible green birds.

RELIGION, SPIRITUALITY & MYSTICISM
·⫻·

LOVE AND DEATH

Behold the flashing waters
  A cloven dancing jet,
That from the milk-white marble
  For ever foam and fret;
Far off in drowsy valleys
  Where the meadow saffrons blow,
The feet of summer dabble
  In their coiling calm and slow.
The banks are worn forever
  By a people sadly gay:
A Titan, with loud laughter,
  Made them of fire clay.
Go ask the springing flowers,
  And the flowing air above,
What are the twin-born waters,
  And they'll answer Death and Love.

With wreaths of withered flowers
  Two lonely spirits wait,
With wreaths of withered flowers
  'Fore paradise's gate.
They may not pass the portal,
  Poor earth-enkindled pair,
Though sad is many a spirit
  To pass and leave them there
Still staring at their flowers,

That dull and faded are.
If one should rise beside thee,
    The other is not far.
Go ask the youngest angel,
    She will say with bated breath,
By the door of Mary's garden
    Are the spirits Love and Death.

ANASHUYA AND VIJAYA

A little Indian temple in the Golden Age. Around it a garden; around that the forest. ANASHUYA, *the young priestess, kneeling within the temple.*

ANASHUYA

Send peace on all the lands and flickering corn –
O, may tranquillity walk by his elbow
When wandering in the forest, if he love
No other. – Hear, and may the indolent flocks
Be plentiful. – And if he love another,
May panthers end him. – Hear, and load our king
With wisdom hour by hour. – May we two stand,
When we are dead, beyond the setting suns,
A little from the other shades apart,
With mingling hair, and play upon one lute.

VIJAYA [*entering and throwing a lily at her*]
Hail! hail, my Anashuya.

ANASHUYA

                              No: be still.
I, priestess of this temple, offer up
Prayers for the land.

VIJAYA

                              I will wait here, Amrita.

ANASHUYA
By mighty Brahma's ever rustling robe,
Who is Amrita? Sorrow of all sorrows!
Another fills your mind.

VIJAYA

My mother's name.

ANASHUYA [*sings, coming out of the temple*]
A sad, sad thought went by me slowly:
Sigh, O you little stars! O, sigh and shake your
blue apparel!
The sad, sad thought has gone from me now wholly:
Sing, O you little stars! O, sing and raise your
rapturous carol
To mighty Brahma, he who made you many as
the sands,
And laid you on the gates of evening with his
quiet hands.
[*Sits down on the steps of the temple.*]

Vijaya, I have brought my evening rice;
The sun has laid his chin on the gray wood,
Weary, with all his poppies gathered round him.

VIJAYA
The hour when Kama, full of sleepy laughter,

Rises, and showers abroad his fragrant arrows,
Piercing the twilight with their murmuring barbs.

ANASHUYA
See how the sacred old flamingoes come,
Painting with shadow all the marble steps:
Aged and wise, they seek their wonted perches
Within the temple, devious walking, made
To wander by their melancholy minds.
Yon tall one eyes my supper; swiftly chase him
Far, far away. I named him after you.
He is a famous fisher; hour by hour
He ruffles with his bill the minnowed streams.
Ah! there he snaps my rice. I told you so.
Now cuff him off. He's off! A kiss for you,
Because you saved my rice. Have you no thanks?

VIJAYA [*sings*]
Sing you of her, O first few stars,
Whom Brahma, touching with his finger, praises, for
    you hold
The van of wandering quiet; ere you be too calm
    and old,
Sing, turning in your cars,
Sing, till you raise your hands and sigh, and from
    your car heads peer,
With all your whirling hair, and drop many an
    azure tear.

ANASHUYA
What know the pilots of the stars of tears?

VIJAYA
Their faces are all worn, and in their eyes
Flashes the fire of sadness, for they see
The icicles that famish all the north,
Where men lie frozen in the glimmering snow;
And in the flaming forests cower the lion
And lioness, with all their whimpering cubs;
And, ever pacing on the verge of things,
The phantom, Beauty, in a mist of tears;
While we alone have round us woven woods,
And feel the softness of each other's hand,
Amrita, while—

ANASHUYA [*going away from him*]
                              Ah me, you love another,
[*Bursting into tears.*]
And may some dreadful ill befall her quick!

VIJAYA
I loved another; now I love no other.
Among the mouldering of ancient woods
You live, and on the village border she,
With her old father the blind wood-cutter;
I saw her standing in her door but now.

ANASHUYA
Vijaya, swear to love her never more,

VIJAYA
Ay, ay.

ANASHUYA
      Swear by the parents of the gods,
Dread oath, who dwell on sacred Himalay,
On the far Golden Peak; enormous shapes,
Who still were old when the great sea was young
On their vast faces mystery and dreams;
Their hair along the mountains rolled and filled
From year to year by the unnumbered nests
Of aweless birds, and round their stirless feet
The joyous flocks of deer and antelope,
Who never hear the unforgiving hound.
Swear!

VIJAYA
      By the parents of the gods, I swear.

ANASHUYA [*sings*]
I have forgiven, O new star!
Maybe you have not heard of us, you have come forth
   so newly,
You hunter of the fields afar!

Ah, you will know my loved one by his hunter's
arrows truly,
Shoot on him shafts of quietness, that he may
ever keep
An inner laughter, and may kiss his hands to me
in sleep.

Farewell, Vijaya. Nay, no word, no word;
I, priestess of this temple, offer up
Prayers for the land.

[VIJAYA *goes.*]
                              O Brahma, guard in sleep
The merry lambs and the complacent kine,
The flies below the leaves, and the young mice
In the tree roots, and all the sacred flocks
Of red flamingo; and my love, Vijaya;
And may no restless fay with fidget finger
Trouble his sleeping: give him dreams of me.

THE INDIAN UPON GOD

I passed along the water's edge below the
    humid trees,
My spirit rocked in evening light, the rushes round
    my knees,
My spirit rocked in sleep and sighs; and saw the
    moorfowl pace
All dripping on a grassy slope, and saw them cease
    to chase
Each other round in circles, and heard the
    eldest speak:
*Who holds the world between His bill and made us
    strong or weak*
Is an undying moorfowl, and He lives beyond the sky.
The rains are from His dripping wing, the
    moonbeams from His eye.
I passed a little further on and heard a lotus talk:
Who made the world and ruleth it, He hangeth on
    a stalk,
For I am in His image made, and all this tinkling tide
Is but a sliding drop of rain between His petals wide.
A little way within the gloom a roebuck raised his eyes
Brimful of starlight, and he said: *The Stamper of*
    the Skies,
He is a gentle roebuck; for how else, I pray, could He
Conceive a thing so sad and soft, a gentle thing
    like me?

I passed a little further on and heard a peacock say:
*Who made the grass and made the worms and made
my feathers gay,*
*He is a monstrous peacock, and He waveth all
the night*
*His languid tail above us, lit with myriad spots
of light.*

THE INDIAN TO HIS LOVE

The island dreams under the dawn
And great boughs drop tranquillity;
The peahens dance on a smooth lawn,
A parrot sways upon a tree,
Raging at his own image in the enamelled sea.

Here we will moor our lonely ship
And wander ever with woven hands,
Murmuring softly lip to lip,
Along the grass, along the sands,
Murmuring how far away are the unquiet lands:

How we alone of mortals are
Hid under quiet bows apart,
While our love grows an Indian star,
A meteor of the burning heart,
One with the tide that gleams, the wings that gleam
    and dart,

The heavy boughs, the burnished dove
That moans and sighs a hundred days:
How when we die our shades will rove,
When eve has hushed the feathered ways,
With vapoury footsole among the water's
    drowsy blaze.

THE BALLAD OF FATHER GILLIGAN

The old priest Peter Gilligan
Was weary night and day;
For half his flock were in their beds,
Or under green sods lay.

Once, while he nodded on a chair,
At the moth-hour of eve,
Another poor man sent for him,
And he began to grieve.

"I have no rest, nor joy, nor peace,
"For people die and die";
And after cried he, "God forgive!
"My body spake, not I!"

He knelt, and leaning on the chair
He prayed and fell asleep;
And the moth-hour went from the fields,
And stars began to peep.

They slowly into millions grew,
And leaves shook in the wind;
And God covered the world with shade,
And whispered to mankind.

Upon the time of sparrow chirp
When the moths came once more,
The old priest Peter Gilligan
Stood upright on the floor.

"Mavrone, mavrone! the man has died,
"While I slept on the chair";
He roused his horse out of its sleep,
And rode with little care.

He rode now as he never rode,
By rocky lane and fen;
The sick man's wife opened the door:
"Father! you come again!"

"And is the poor man dead?" he cried,
"He died an hour ago,"
The old priest Peter Gilligan
In grief swayed to and fro.

"When you were gone, he turned and died
"As merry as a bird."
The old priest Peter Gilligan
He knelt him at that word.

"He who hath made the night of stars
"For souls, who tire and bleed,
"Sent one of His great angels down
"To help me in my need.

"He who is wrapped in purple robes,
"With planets in His care,
"Had pity on the least of things
"Asleep upon a chair."

THE TWO TREES

Beloved, gaze in thine own heart,
The holy tree is growing there;
From joy the holy branches start,
And all the trembling flowers they bear.
The changing colours of its fruit
Have dowered the stars with merry light;
The surety of its hidden root
Has planted quiet in the night;
The shaking of its leafy head
Has given the waves their melody,
And made my lips and music wed,
Murmuring a wizard song for thee.
There, through bewildered branches, go
Winged Loves borne on in gentle strife,
Tossing and tossing to and fro
The flaming circle of our life.
When looking on their shaken hair,
And dreaming how they dance and dart,
Thine eyes grow full of tender care:
Beloved, gaze in thine own heart.

Gaze no more in the bitter glass
The demons, with their subtle guile,
Lift up before us when they pass,
Or only gaze a little while;
For there a fatal image grows,

With broken boughs, and blackened leaves,
And roots half hidden under snows
Driven by a storm that ever grieves.
For all things turn to barrenness
In the dim glass the demons hold,
The glass of outer weariness,
Made when God slept in times of old.
There, through the broken branches, go
The ravens of unresting thought;
Peering and flying to and fro
To see men's souls bartered and bought.
When they are heard upon the wind,
And when they shake their wings; alas!
Thy tender eyes grow all unkind:
Gaze no more in the bitter glass.

THE MOODS

Time drops in decay,
Like a candle burnt out,
And the mountains and woods
Have their day, have their day;
What one in the rout
Of the fire-born moods,
Has fallen away?

BREASAL THE FISHERMAN

Although you hide in the ebb and flow
Of the pale tide when the moon has set,
The people of coming days will know
About the casting out of my net,
And how you have leaped times out of mind
Over the little silver cords,
And think that you were hard and unkind,
And blame you with many bitter words.

INTO THE TWILIGHT

Out-worn heart, in a time out-worn,
Come clear of the nets of wrong and right;
Laugh heart again in the gray twilight,
Sigh, heart, again in the dew of the morn.

Your mother Eire is always young,
Dew ever shining and twilight gray;
Though hope fall from you and love decay,
Burning in fires of a slanderous tongue.

Come, heart, where hill is heaped upon hill:
For there the mystical brotherhood
Of sun and moon and hollow and wood
And river and stream work out their will;

And God stands winding His lonely horn,
And time and the world are ever in flight;
And love is less kind than the gray twilight,
And hope is less dear than the dew of the morn.

THE SECRET ROSE

Far off, most secret, and inviolate Rose,
Enfold me in my hour of hours; where those
Who sought thee in the Holy Sepulchre,
Or in the wine vat, dwell beyond the stir
And tumult of defeated dreams; and deep
Among pale eyelids, heavy with the sleep
Men have named beauty. Thy great leaves enfold
The ancient beards, the helms of ruby and gold
Of the crowned Magi; and the king whose eyes
Saw the Pierced Hands and Road of elder rise
In druid vapour and make the torches dim;
Till vain frenzy awoke and he died; and him
Who met Fand walking among flaming dew
By a gray shore where the wind never blew
And lost the world and Emer for a kiss;
And him who drove the gods out of their liss,
And till a hundred morns had flowered red,
Feasted and wept the barrows of his dead;
And the proud dreaming king who flung the crown
And sorrow away, and calling hard and clown
Dwelt among wine-stained wanderers in deep woods;
And him who sold tillage, and house, and goods,
And sought through lands and islands
    numberless years,
Until he found with laughter and with tears,
A woman, of so shining loveliness,

That men threshed corn at midnight by a tress,
A little stolen tress. I, too, await
The hour of thy great wind of love and hate.
When shall the stars be blown about the sky,
Like the sparks blown out of a smithy, and die?
Surely thine hour has come, thy great wind blows,
Far off, most secret, and inviolate Rose?

THE TRAVAIL OF PASSION

When the flaming lute-thronged angelic door is wide;
When an immortal passion breathes in mortal clay;
Our hearts endure the scourge, the plaited thorns,
    the way
Crowded with bitter faces, the wounds in palm
    and side,
The hyssop-heavy sponge, the flowers by
    Kidron stream:
We will bend down and loosen our hair over you,
That it may drop faint perfume, and be heavy
    with dew,
Lilies of death-pale hope, roses of passionate dream

AEDH PLEADS WITH THE
ELEMENTAL POWERS

The Powers whose name and shape no living
    creature knows
Have pulled the Immortal Rose;
And though the Seven Lights bowed in their dance
    and wept,
The Polar Dragon slept,
His heavy rings uncoiled from glimmering deep
    to deep:
When will he wake from sleep?

Great Powers of falling wave and wind and windy fire,
With your harmonious choir
Encircle her I love and sing her into peace,
That my old care may cease;
Unfold your flaming wings and cover out of sight
The nets of day and night.

Dim Powers of drowsy thought, let her no longer be
Like the pale cup of the sea,
When winds have gathered and sun and moon
    burned dim
Above its cloudy rim;
But let a gentle silence wrought with music flow
Whither her footsteps go.

THE MOUNTAIN TOMB

Pour wine and dance if Manhood still have pride,
Bring roses if the rose be yet in bloom;
The cataract smokes upon the mountain side,
Our Father Rosicross is in his tomb.

Pull down the blinds, bring fiddle and clarionet
That there be no foot silent in the room
Nor mouth from kissing, nor from wine unwet,
Our Father Rosicross is in his tomb.

In vain, in vain; the cataract still cries
The everlasting taper lights the gloom;
All wisdom shut into his onyx eyes
Our Father Rosicross sleeps in his tomb.

THE COLD HEAVEN

Suddenly I saw the cold and rook-delighting Heaven
That seemed as though ice burned and was but the
    more ice,
And thereupon imagination and heart were driven
So wild, that every casual thought of that and this
Vanished, and left but memories, that should be out
    of season
With the hot blood of youth, of love crossed long ago;
And I took all the blame out of all sense and reason,
Until I cried and trembled and rocked to and fro,
Riddled with light. Ah! when the ghost begins
    to quicken,
Confusion of the death-bed over, is it sent
Out naked on the roads, as the books say, and stricken
By the injustice of the skies for punishment?

THE MAGI

Now as at all times I can see in the mind's eye,
In their stiff, painted clothes, the pale unsatisfied ones
Appear and disappear in the blue depth of the sky
With all their ancient faces like rain-beaten stones,
And all their helms of silver hovering side by side,
And all their eyes still fixed, hoping to find once more,
Being by Calvary's turbulence unsatisfied,
The uncontrollable mystery on the bestial floor.

SOLOMON AND THE WITCH

And thus declared that Arab lady:
"Last night, where under the wild moon
On grassy mattress I had laid me,
Within my arms great Solomon,
I suddenly cried out in a strange tongue
Not his, not mine."

              And he that knew
All sounds by bird or angel sung
Answered: "A crested cockerel crew
Upon a blossoming apple bough
Three hundred years before the Fall,
And never crew again till now,
And would not now but that he thought,
Chance being at one with Choice at last,
All that the brigand apple brought
And this foul world were dead at last.
He that crowed out eternity
Thought to have crowed it in again.
A lover with a spider's eye
Will find out some appropriate pain,
Aye, though all passion's in the glance,
For every nerve: lover tests lover
With cruelties of Choice and Chance;
And when at last that murder's over
Maybe the bride-bed brings despair
For each an imagined image brings

And finds a real image there;
Yet the world ends when these two things,
Though several, are a single light,
When oil and wick are burned in one;
Therefore a blessed moon last night
Gave Sheba to her Solomon."

"Yet the world stays":
                    "If that be so,
Your cockerel found us in the wrong
Although he thought it worth a crow.
Maybe an image is too strong
Or maybe is not strong enough."

"The night has fallen; not a sound
In the forbidden sacred grove
Unless a petal hit the ground,
Nor any human sight within it
But the crushed grass where we have lain;
And the moon is wilder every minute.
Oh, Solomon! let us try again."

DEMON AND BEAST

For certain minutes at the least
That crafty demon and that loud beast
That plague me day and night
Ran out of my sight;
Though I had long pernned in the gyre,
Between my hatred and desire,
I saw my freedom won
And all laugh in the sun.

The glittering eyes in a death's head
Of old Luke Wadding's portrait said
Welcome, and the Ormonds all
Nodded upon the wall,
And even Stafford smiled as though
It made him happier to know
I understood his plan;
Now that the loud beast ran
There was no portrait in the Gallery
But beckoned to sweet company,
For all men's thoughts grew clear
Being dear as mine are dear.

But soon a tear-drop started up
For aimless joy had made me stop
Beside the little lake
To watch a white gull take

A bit of bread thrown up into the air;
Now gyring down and pernning there
He splashed where an absurd
Portly green-pated bird
Shook off the water from his back;
Being no more demoniac
A stupid happy creature
Could rouse my whole nature.

Yet I am certain as can be
That every natural victory
Belongs to beast or demon,
That never yet had freeman
Right mastery of natural things,
And that mere growing old, that brings
Chilled blood, this sweetness brought;
Yet have no dearer thought
Than that I may find out a way
To make it linger half a day.

O what a sweetness strayed
Through barren Thebaid,
Or by the Mareotic sea
When that exultant Anthony
And twice a thousand more
Starved upon the shore
And withered to a bag of bones:
What had the Caesars but their thrones?

ALL SOULS' NIGHT

'Tis All Souls' Night and the great Christ Church bell,
And many a lesser bell, sound through the room,
For it is now midnight;
And two long glasses brimmed with muscatel
Bubble upon the table. A ghost may come,
For it is a ghost's right,
His element is so fine
Being sharpened by his death,
To drink from the wine-breath
While our gross palates drink from the whole wine.

I need some mind that, if the cannon sound
From every quarter of the world, can stay
Wound in mind's pondering,
As mummies in the mummy-cloth are wound;
Because I have a marvellous thing to say,
A certain marvellous thing
None but the living mock,
Though not for sober ear;
It may be all that hear
Should laugh and weep an hour upon the clock.

H——'s the first I call. He loved strange thought
And knew that sweet extremity of pride
That's called platonic love,
And that to such a pitch of passion wrought

Nothing could bring him, when his lady died,
Anodyne for his love.
Words were but wasted breath;
One dear hope had he:
The inclemency
Of that or the next winter would be death.

Two thoughts were so mixed up I could not tell
Whether of her or God he thought the most,
But think that his mind's eye,
When upward turned, on one sole image fell,
And that a slight companionable ghost,
Wild with divinity,
Had so lit up the whole
Immense miraculous house,
The Bible promised us,
It seemed a gold-fish swimming in a bowl.

On Florence Emery I call the next,
Who finding the first wrinkles on a face
Admired and beautiful,
And knowing that the future would be vexed
With 'minished beauty, multiplied commonplace,
Preferred to teach a school,
Away from neighbour or friend
Among dark skins, and there
Permit foul years to wear
Hidden from eyesight to the unnoticed end.

Before that end much had she ravelled out
From a discourse in figurative speech
By some learned Indian
On the soul's journey. How it is whirled about,
Wherever the orbit of the moon can reach,
Until it plunged into the sun;
And there free and yet fast,
Being both Chance and Choice,
Forget its broken toys
And sink into its own delight at last.

And I call up MacGregor from the grave,
For in my first hard springtime we were friends,
Although of late estranged.
I thought him half a lunatic, half knave,
And told him so, but friendship never ends;
And what if mind seem changed,
And it seem changed with the mind,
When thoughts rise up unbid
On generous things that he did
And I grow half contented to be blind.

He had much industry at setting out,
Much boisterous courage, before loneliness
Had driven him crazed;
For meditations upon unknown thought
Make human intercourse grow less and less;
They are neither paid nor praised.

But he'd object to the host,
The glass because my glass;
A ghost-lover he was
And may have grown more arrogant being a ghost.

But names are nothing. What matter who it be,
So that his elements have grown so fine
The fume of muscatel
Can give his sharpened palate ecstasy
No living man can drink from the whole wine.
I have mummy truths to tell
Whereat the living mock,
Though not for sober ear,
For maybe all that hear
Should laugh and weep an hour upon the clock.

Such thought – such thought have I that hold it tight
Till meditation master all its parts,
Nothing can stay my glance
Until that glance run in the world's despite
To where the damned have howled away their hearts,
And where the blessed dance;
Such thought, that in it bound
I need no other thing
Wound in mind's wandering,
As mummies in the mummy-cloth are wound.

THE WHEEL

Through winter-time we call on spring,
And through the spring on summer call,
And when abounding hedges sing
Declare that winter's best of all;
And after that there's nothing good
Because the spring-time has not come –
Nor know that what disturbs our blood
Is but its longing for the tomb.

THE CAT AND THE MOON

(As sung by the 'First Musician' at different points in the play *The Cat and the Moon*)

The cat went here and there
And the moon spun round like a top,
And the nearest kin of the moon
The creeping cat looked up.
Black Minnaloushe stared at the moon,
For wander and wail as he would
The pure cold light in the sky
Troubled his animal blood.

Minnaloushe runs in the grass,
Lifting his delicate feet.
Do you dance, Minnaloushe, do you dance?
When two close kindred meet
What better than call a dance,
Maybe the moon may learn,
Tired of that courtly fashion,
A new dance turn.

Minnaloushe creeps through the grass
From moonlight place to place
The sacred moon overhead
Has taken a new phase.
Does Minnaloushe know that his pupils

Will pass from change to change,
And that from round to crescent,
From crescent to round they range?
Minnaloushe creeps through the grass
Alone, important and wise,
And lifts to the changing moon
His changing eyes.

THE GIFT OF HARUN-AL-RASHID

Kusta-ben-Luka is my name, I write
To Abd-Al-Rabban; fellow-roysterer once
Now the good Caliph's learned Treasurer,
And for no ear but his.
               Carry this letter
Through the great gallery of the Treasure House
Where banners of the Caliphs hang, night-coloured
But brilliant as the night's embroidery,
And wait war's music; pass the little gallery;
Pass books of learning from Byzantium
Written in gold upon a purple stain,
And pause at last, I was about to say,
At the great book of Sappho's song; but no,
For should you leave my letter there, a boy's
Love-lorn, indifferent hands might come upon it
And let it fall unnoticed to the floor.
Pause at the Treatise of Parmenides
And hide it there, for Caliphs' to world's end
Must keep that perfect, as they keep her song
So great its fame.
                When fitting time has passed
The parchment will disclose to some learned man
A mystery that else had found no chronicler
But the wild Bedouin. Though I approve
Those wanderers that welcomed in their tents
What great Harun-al-Rashid, occupied

With Persian wars or Grecian ambassadors,
Must needs neglect; I cannot hide the truth
That wandering in a desert, featureless
As air under a wing, can give birds' wit.
In after time they will speak much of me
And speak but phantasy. Recall the year
When our beloved Caliph put to death
His Vizir Jaffer for an unknown reason:
"If but the shirt upon my body knew it
I'd tear it off and throw it in the fire."
That speech was all that the town knew, but he
Seemed for a while to have grown young again;
Seemed so on purpose, muttered Jaffer's friends,
That none might know that he was conscience-struck –
But that's a traitor's thought. Enough for me
That in the early summer of the year
The mightiest of the princes of the world
Came to the least considered of his courtiers;
Sat down upon the fountain's marble edge
One hand amid the goldfish in the pool;
And thereupon a colloquy took place
That I commend to all the chroniclers
To show how violent great hearts can lose
Their bitterness and find the honeycomb.

"I have brought a slender bride into the house;
You know the saying, 'Change the bride with spring.'
And she and I, being sunk in happiness,

Cannot endure to think you tread these paths,
When evening stirs the jasmine, and yet
Are brideless."
                              "I am falling into years."
"But such as you and I do not seem old
Like men who live by habit. Every day
I ride with falcon to the river's edge
Or carry the ringed mail upon my back,
Or court a woman; neither enemy,
Game-bird, nor woman does the same thing twice;
And so a hunter carries in the eye
A mimicry of youth. Can poet's thought
That springs from body and in body falls
Like this pure jet, now lost amid blue sky,
Now bathing lily leaf and fishes' scale,
Be mimicry?"
                              "What matter if our souls
Are nearer to the surface of the body
Than souls that start no game and turn no rhyme!
The soul's own youth and not the body's youth
Shows through our lineaments. My candle's bright,
My lantern is too loyal not to show
That it was made in your great father's reign."

"And yet the jasmine season warms our blood."

"Great prince, forgive the freedom of my speech;
You think that love has seasons, and you think

That if the spring bear off what the spring gave
The heart need suffer no defeat; but I
Who have accepted the Byzantine faith,
That seems unnatural to Arabian minds,
Think when I choose a bride I choose for ever;
And if her eye should not grow bright for mine
Or brighten only for some younger eye,
My heart could never turn from daily ruin,
Nor find a remedy."

                "But what if I
Have lit upon a woman, who so shares
Your thirst for those old crabbed mysteries,
So strains to look beyond our life, an eye
That never knew that strain would scarce seem bright,
And yet herself can seem youth's very fountain,
Being all brimmed with life."

               "Were it but true
I would have found the best that life can give,
Companionship in those mysterious things
That make a man's soul or a woman's soul
Itself and not some other soul."

                  "That love
Must needs be in this life and in what follows
Unchanging and at peace, and it is right
Every philosopher should praise that love.
But I being none can praise its opposite.
It makes my passion stronger but to think
Like passion stirs the peacock and his mate,

The wild stag and the doe; that mouth to mouth
Is a man's mockery of the changeless soul."
And thereupon his bounty gave what now
Can shake more blossom from autumnal chill
Than all my bursting springtime knew. A girl
Perched in some window of her mother's house
Had watched my daily passage to and fro;
Had heard impossible history of my past;
Imagined some impossible history
Lived at my side; thought Time's disfiguring touch
Gave but more reason for a woman's care.
Yet was it love of me, or was it love
Of the stark mystery that has dazed my sight,
Perplexed her phantasy and planned her care?
Or did the torchlight of that mystery
Pick out my features in such light and shade
Two contemplating passions chose one theme
Through sheer bewilderment? She had not paced
The garden paths, nor counted up the rooms,
Before she had spread a book upon her knees
And asked about the pictures or the text;
And often those first days I saw her stare
On old dry writing in a learned tongue,
On old dry faggots that could never please
The extravagance of spring; or move a hand
As if that writing or the figured page
Were some dear cheek.

               Upon a moonless night

I sat where I could watch her sleeping form,
And wrote by candle-light; but her form moved,
And fearing that my light disturbed her sleep
I rose that I might screen it with a cloth.
I heard her voice, "Turn that I may expound
What's bowed your shoulder and made pale
        your cheek";
And saw her sitting upright on the bed;
Or was it she that spoke or some great Djinn?
I say that a Djinn spoke. A live-long hour
She seemed the learned man and I the child;
Truths without father came, truths that no book
Of all the uncounted books that I have read,
Nor thought out of her mind or mine begot,
Self-born, high-born, and solitary truths,
Those terrible implacable straight lines
Drawn through the wandering vegetative dream,
Even those truths that when my bones are dust
Must drive the Arabian host.

                        The voice grew still,
And she lay down upon her bed and slept,
But woke at the first gleam of day, rose up
And swept the house and sang about her work
In childish ignorance of all that passed.

A dozen nights of natural sleep, and then
When the full moon swam to its greatest height

She rose, and with her eyes shut fast in sleep
Walked through the house. Unnoticed and unfelt
I wrapped her in a heavy hooded cloak, and she,
Half running, dropped at the first ridge of the desert
And there marked out those emblems on the sand
That day by day I study and marvel at,
With her white finger. I led her home asleep
And once again she rose and swept the house
In childish ignorance of all that passed.
Even today, after some seven years
When maybe thrice in every moon her mouth
Murmured the wisdom of the desert Djinns,
She keeps that ignorance, nor has she now
That first unnatural interest in my books.
It seems enough that I am there; and yet,
Old fellow student, whose most patient ear
Heard all the anxiety of my passionate youth,
It seems I must buy knowledge with my peace.
What if she lose her ignorance and so
Dream that I love her only for the voice,
That every gift and every word of praise
Is but a payment for that midnight voice
That is to age what milk is to a child!
Were she to lose her love, because she had lost
Her confidence in mine, or even lose
Its first simplicity, love, voice and all,
All my fine feathers would be plucked away
And I left shivering. The voice has drawn

A quality of wisdom from her love's
Particular quality. The signs and shapes;
All those abstractions that you fancied were
From the great Treatise of Parmenides;
All, all those gyres and cubes and midnight things
Are but a new expression of her body
Drunk with the bitter sweetness of her youth.
And now my utmost mystery is out.
A woman's beauty is a storm-tossed banner;
Under it wisdom stands, and I alone –
Of all Arabia's lovers I alone –
Nor dazzled by the embroidery, nor lost
In the confusion of its night-dark folds,
Can hear the armed man speak.

LEGENDARY FIGURES
& FAERY LORE
·≫✳≪·

THE MADNESS OF KING GOLL

I sat on cushioned otter skin:
My word was law from Ith to Emen,
And shook at Invar Amargin
The hearts of the world-troubling seamen.
And drove tumult and war away
From girl and boy and man and beast;
The fields grew fatter day by day,
The wild fowl of the air increased;
And every ancient Ollave said,
While he bent down his fading head,
"He drives away the Northern cold."
*They will not hush, the leaves a-flutter round me, the
    beech leaves old.*

I sat and mused and drank sweet wine;
A herdsman came from inland valleys,
Crying, the pirates drove his swine
To fill their dark-beaked hollow galleys.
I called my battle-breaking men,
And my loud brazen battle-cars
From rolling vale and rivery glen,
And under the blinking of the stars
Fell on the pirates by the deep,
And hurled them in the gulph of sleep:
These hands won many a torque of gold.
*They will not hush, the leaves a-flutter round me, the
    beech leaves old.*

But slowly, as I shouting slew
And trampled in the bubbling mire,
In my most secret spirit grew
A whirling and a wandering fire:
I stood: keen stars above me shone,
Around me shone keen eyes of men:
I laughed aloud and hurried on
By rocky shore and rushy fen;
I laughed because birds fluttered by,
And starlight gleamed, and clouds flew high,
And rushes waved and waters rolled.
*They will not hush, the leaves a-flutter round me, the
    beech leaves old.*

And now I wander in the woods
When summer gluts the golden bees,
Or in autumnal solitudes
Arise the leopard-coloured trees;
Or when along the wintry strands
The cormorants shiver on their rocks;
I wander on, and wave my hands,
And sing, and shake my heavy locks.
The gray wolf knows me; by one ear
I lead along the woodland deer;
The hares run by me growing bold.
*They will not hush, the leaves a-flutter round me, the
    beech leaves old.*

I came upon a little town,
That slumbered in the harvest moon,
And passed a-tiptoe up and down,
Murmuring, to a fitful tune,
How I have followed, night and day,
A tramping of tremendous feet,
And saw where this old tympan lay,
Deserted on a doorway seat,
And bore it to the woods with me;
Of some unhuman misery
Our married voiced wildly trolled.
*They will not hush, the leaves a-flutter round me, the
    beech leaves old.*

I sang how, when day's toil is done,
Orchil shakes out her long dark hair
That hides away the dying sun
And sheds faint odours through the air:
When my hand passed from wire to wire
It quenched, with sound like falling dew,
The whirling and the wandering fire;
But lift a mournful ulalu,
For the kind wires are torn and still,
And I must wander wood and hill
Through summer's heat and winter's cold.
*They will not hush, the leaves a-flutter round me, the
    beech leaves old.*

THE STOLEN CHILD

Where dips the rocky highland
Of Sleuth Wood in the lake,
There lies a leafy island
Where flapping herons wake
The drowsy water rats;
There we've hid our faery vats,
Full of berries,
And of reddest stolen cherries.
Come away, O human child!
To the waters and the wild
With a faery, hand in hand,
For the world's more full of weeping than you
*   can understand.*

Where the wave of moonlight glosses
The dim gray sands with light,
Far off by furthest Rosses
We foot it all the night,
Weaving olden dances,
Mingling hands and mingling glances
Till the moon has taken flight;
To and fro we leap
And chase the frothy bubbles,
While the world is full of troubles
And is anxious in its sleep.

Come away, O human child!
To the waters and the wild
With a faery, hand in hand,
For the world's more full of weeping than you
    can understand.

Where the wandering water gushes
From the hills above Glen-Car,
In pools among the rushes
That scarce could bathe a star,
We seek for slumbering trout
And whispering in their ears
Give them unquiet dreams;
Leaning softly out
From ferns that drop their tears
Over the young streams,
Come away, O human child!
To the waters and the wild
With a faery, hand in hand,
For the world's more full of weeping than you
    can understand.

Away with us he's going,
The solemn-eyed:
He'll hear no more the lowing
Of the calves on the warm hillside
Or the kettle on the hob
Sing peace into his breast,

Or see the brown mice bob
Round and round the oatmeal-chest.
For he comes, the human child,
To the waters and the wild
With a faery, hand in hand,
From a world more full of weeping than he
    can understand.

TO AN ISLE IN THE WATER

Shy one, shy one,
Shy one of my heart,
She moves in the firelight
Pensively apart.

She carries in the dishes,
And lays them in a row.
To an isle in the water
With her would I go.

She carries in the candles,
And lights the curtained room,
Shy in the doorway
And shy in the gloom;

And shy as a rabbit,
Helpful and shy.
To an isle in the water
With her would I fly.

THE WANDERINGS OF OISIN

Book I

S. PATRICK
You who are bent, and bald, and blind,
With a heavy heart and a wandering mind,
Have known three centuries, poets sing,
Of dalliance with a demon thing.

OISIN
Sad to remember, sick with years,
The swift innumerable spears,
The horsemen with their floating hair,
And bowls of barley, honey, and wine,
And feet of maidens dancing in tune,
And the white body that lay by mine;
But the tale, though words be lighter than air,
Must live to be old like the wandering moon.

Caolte, and Conan, and Finn were there,
When we followed a deer with our baying hounds,
With Bran, Sgeolan, and Lomair,
And passing the Firbolgs' burial mounds,
Came to the cairn-heaped grassy hill
Where passionate Maeve is stony still;
And found on the dove-gray edge of the sea
A pearl-pale, high-born lady, who rode

On a horse with bridle of findrinny;
And like a sunset were her lips,
A stormy sunset on doomed ships;
A citron colour gloomed in her hair,
But down to her feet white vesture flowed,
And with the glimmering crimson glowed
Of many a figured embroidery;
And it was bound with a pearl-pale shell
That wavered like the summer streams,
As her soft bosom rose and fell.

S. PATRICK
You are still wrecked among heathen dreams.

OISIN
"Why do you wind no horn?" she said.
"And every hero droop his head?
"The hornless deer is not more sad
"That many a peaceful moment had,
"More sleek than any granary mouse,
"In his own leafy forest house
"Among the waving fields of fern:
"The hunting of heroes should be glad."

"O pleasant woman," answered Finn,
"We think on Oscar's pencilled urn,
"And on the heroes lying slain,
On Gavra's raven-covered plain;

"But where are your noble kith and kin,
"And from what country do you ride?"

"My father and my mother are
"Aengus and Adene, my own name
"Niamh, and my country far
"Beyond the tumbling of this tide."

"What dream came with you that you came
"Through bitter tide on foam wet feet?
"Did your companion wander away
"From where the birds of Aengus wing?"

She said, with laughter tender and sweet:
"I have not yet, war-weary king,
"Been spoken of with any one;
"Yet now I choose, for these four feet
"Ran through the foam and ran to this
"That I might have your son to kiss."

"Were there no better than my son
"That you through all that foam should run?"

"I loved no man, though kings besought
"Love, till the Danaan poets brought
"Rhyme, that rhymed to Oisin's name,
"And now I am dizzy with the thought
"Of all that wisdom and the fame

"Of battles broken by his hands,
"Of stories builded by his words
"That are like coloured Asian birds
"At evening in their rainless lands."

O Patrick, by your brazen bell,
There was no limb of mine but fell
Into a desperate gulph of love!
"You only will I wed," I cried,
"And I will make a thousand songs,
"And set your name all names above.
"And captives bound with leathern thongs
"Shall kneel and praise you, one by one,
"At evening in my western dun."

"O Oisin, mount by me and ride
"To shores by the wash of the tremulous tide,
"Where men have heaped no burial mounds,
"And the days pass by like a wayward tune,
"Where broken faith has never been known,
"And the blushes of first love never have flown;
"And there I will give you a hundred hounds;
"No mightier creatures bay at the moon;
"And a hundred robes of murmuring silk,
"And a hundred calves and a hundred sheep
"Whose long wool whiter than sea froth flows,
"And a hundred spears and a hundred bows,
"And oil and wine and honey and milk,

"And always never-anxious sleep;
"While a hundred youths, mighty of limb,
"But knowing nor tumult nor hate nor strife,
"And a hundred maidens, merry as birds,
"Who when they dance to a fitful measure
"Have a speed like the speed of the salmon herds,
"Shall follow your horn and obey your whim,
"And you shall know the Danaan leisure:
"And Niamh be with you for a wife."
Then she sighed gently, "It grows late,
"Music and love and sleep await,
"Where I would be when the white moon climbs
"The red sun falls, and the world grows dim."

And then I mounted and she bound me
With her triumphing arms around me,
And whispering to herself enwound me;
But when the horse had felt my weight,
He shook himself and neighed three times:
Caolte, Conan, and Finn came near,
And wept, and raised their lamenting hands,
And bid me stay, with many a tear;
But we rode out from the human lands.

In what far kingdom do you go,
Ah, Fenians, with the shield and bow?
Or are you phantoms white as snow,
Whose lips had life's most prosperous glow?

O you, with whom in sloping valleys,
Or down the dewy forest alleys,
I chased at morn the flying deer,
With whom I hurled the hurrying spear,
And heard the foemen's bucklers rattle,
And broke the heaving ranks of battle!
And Bran, Sgeolan, and Lomair,
Where are you with your long rough hair?
You go not where the red deer feeds,
Nor tear the foemen from their steeds.

S. PATRICK
Boast not, nor mourn with drooping head
Companions long accurst and dead,
And hounds for centuries dust and air.

OISIN
We galloped over the glossy sea:
I know not if days passed or hours,
And Niamh sang continually
Danaan songs, and their dewy showers
Of pensive laughter, unhuman sound,
Lulled weariness, and softly round
My human sorrow her white arms wound.

We galloped; now a hornless deer
Passed by us, chased by a phantom hound
All pearly white, save one red ear;

And now a maiden rode like the wind
With an apple of gold in her tossing hand;
And a beautiful young man followed behind
With quenchless gaze and fluttering hair.

"Were these two born in the Danaan land,
"Or have they breathed the mortal air?"

"Vex them no longer," Niamh said,
And sighing bowed her gentle head,
And sighing laid the pearly tip
Of one long finger on my lip.

But now the moon like a white rose shone
In the pale west, and the sun's rim sank,
And clouds arrayed their rank on rank
About his fading crimson ball:
The floor of Emen's hosting hall
Was not more level than the sea,
As full of loving phantasy,
And with low murmurs we rode on,
Where many a trumpet-twisted shell
That in immortal silence sleeps
Dreaming of her own melting hues,
Her golds, her ambers, and her blues,
Pierced with soft light the shallowing deeps.

But now a wandering land breeze came
And a far sound of feathery quires;

It seemed to blow from the dying flame,
They seemed to sing in the smouldering fires.
The horse towards the music raced,
Neighing along the lifeless waste;
Like sooty fingers, many a tree
Rose ever out of the warm sea;
And they were trembling ceaselessly,
As though they all were beating time,
Upon the centre of the sun,
To that low laughing woodland rhyme.
And, now our wandering hours were done,
We cantered to the shore, and knew
The reason of the trembling trees:
Round every branch the song-birds flew,
Or clung thereon like swarming bees;
While round the shore a million stood
Like drops of frozen rainbow light,
And pondered in a soft vain mood
Upon their shadows in the tide,
And told the purple deeps their pride,
And murmured snatches of delight;
And on the shores were many boats
With bending sterns and bending bows.

And carven figures on their prows
Of bitterns, and fish-eating stoats,
And swans with their exultant throats:
And where the wood and waters meet

We tied the horse in a leafy clump,
And Niamh blew three merry notes
Out of a little silver trump;
And then an answering whispering flew
Over the bare and woody land,
A whisper of impetuous feet,
And ever nearer, nearer grew;
And from the woods rushed out a band
Of men and maidens, hand in hand,
And singing, singing altogether;
Their brows were white as fragrant milk,
Their cloaks made out of yellow silk,
And trimmed with many a crimson feather:
And when they saw the cloak I wore
Was dim with mire of a mortal shore,
They fingered it and gazed on me
And laughed like murmurs of the sea;
But Niamh with a swift distress
Bid them away and hold their peace;
And when they heard her voice they ran
And knelt them, every maid and man
And kissed, as they would never cease,
Her pearl-pale hand and the hem of her dress.
She bade them bring us to the hall
Where Aengus dreams, from sun to sun,
A Druid dream of the end of days
When the stars are to wane and the world be done.

They led us by long and shadowy ways
Where drops of dew in myriads fall,
And tangled creepers every hour
Blossom in some new crimson flower,
And once a sudden laughter sprang
From all their lips, and once they sang
Together, while the dark woods rang,
And made in all their distant parts,
With boom of bees in honey marts,
A rumour of delighted hearts.
And once a maiden by my side
Gave me a harp, and bid me sing,
And touch the laughing silver string;
But when I sang of human joy
A sorrow wrapped each merry face,
And, Patrick! by your beard, they wept,
Until one came, a tearful boy;
"A sadder creature never stept
"Than this strange human bard," he cried;
And caught the silver harp away,
And, weeping over the white strings, hurled
It down in a leaf-hid, hollow place
That kept dim waters from the sky;
And each one said, with a long, long sigh,
"O saddest harp in all the world,
"Sleep there till the moon and the stars die!"

And now still sad we came to where
A beautiful young man dreamed within
A house of wattles, clay, and skin;
One hand upheld his beardless chin,
And one a sceptre flashing out
Wild flames of red and gold and blue,
Like to a merry wandering rout
Of dancers leaping in the air;
And men and maidens knelt them there
And showed their eyes with teardrops dim,
And with low murmurs prayed to him,
And kissed the sceptre with red lips,
And touched it with their finger-tips.

He held that flashing sceptre up.
"Joy drowns the twilight in the dew,
"And fills with stars night's purple cup,
"And wakes the sluggard seeds of corn,
"And stirs the young kid's budding horn.
"And makes the infant ferns unwrap,
"And for the peewit paints his cap,
"And rolls along the unwieldy sun,
"And makes the little planets run:
"And if joy were not on the earth,
"There were an end of change and birth,
"And earth and heaven and hell would die,
"And in some gloomy barrow lie
"Folded like a frozen fly;

"Then mock at Death and Time with glances
"And wavering arms and wandering dances.

"Men's hearts of old were drops of flame
"That from the saffron morning came,
"Or drops of silver joy that fell
"Out of the moon's pale twisted shell;
"But now hearts cry that hearts are slaves,
"And toss and turn in narrow caves;
"But here there is nor law nor rule,
"Nor have hands held a weary tool;
"And here there is nor Change nor Death,
"But only kind and merry breath,
"For joy is God and God is joy."
With one long glance on maid and boy
And the pale blossom of the moon,
He fell into a Druid swoon.

And in a wild and sudden dance
We mocked at Time and Fate and Chance
And swept out of the wattled hall
And came to where the dewdrops fall
Among the foamdrops of the sea,
And there we hushed the revelry;
And, gathering on our brows a frown,
Bent all our swaying bodies down,
And to the waves that glimmer by
That sloping green De Danaan sod

Sang "God is joy and joy is God.
"And things that have grown sad are wicked,
"And things that fear the dawn of the morrow
"Or the gray wandering osprey Sorrow."

We danced to where in the winding thicket
The damask roses, bloom on bloom,
Like crimson meteors hang in the gloom,
And bending over them softly said,
Bending over them in the dance,
With a swift and friendly glance
From dewy eyes: "Upon the dead
"Fall the leaves of other roses,
"On the dead dim earth encloses:
"But never, never on our graves,
"Heaped beside the glimmering waves,
"Shall fall the leaves of damask roses.
"For neither Death nor Change comes near us,
"And all listless hours fear us,
"And we fear no dawning morrow,
"Nor the gray wandering osprey Sorrow."

The dance wound through the windless woods;
The ever-summered solitudes;
Until the tossing arms grew still
Upon the woody central hill;
And, gathered in a panting band,
We flung on high each waving hand,

And sang unto the starry broods:
In our raised eyes there flashed a glow
Of milky brightness to and fro
As thus our song arose: "You stars,
"Across your wandering ruby cars
"Shake the loose reins: you slaves of God
"He rules you with an iron rod,
"He holds you with an iron bond,
"Each one woven to the other,
"Each one woven to his brother
"Like bubbles in a frozen pond;
"But we in a lonely land abide
"Unchainable as the dim tide,
"With hearts that know nor law nor rule,
"And hands that hold no wearisome tool
"Folded in love that fears no morrow,
"Nor the gray wandering osprey Sorrow."

O Patrick! for a hundred years
I chased upon that woody shore
The deer, the badger, and the boar.
O Patrick! for a hundred years
At evening on the glimmering sands,
Beside the piled-up hunting spears,
These now outworn and withered hands
Wrestled among the island bands.
O Patrick! for a hundred years
We went a-fishing in long boats

With bending sterns and bending bows,
And carven figures on their prows
Of bitterns and fish-eating stoats.
O Patrick! for a hundred years
The gentle Niamh was my wife;
But now two things devour my life;
The things that most of all I hate;
Fasting and prayers.

S. PATRICK
                    Tell on.

OISIN
                    Yes, yes,
For these were ancient Oisin's fate
Loosed long ago from heaven's gate,
For his last days to lie in wait.

When one day by the tide I stood,
I found in that forgetfulness
Of dreamy foam a staff of wood
From some dead warrior's broken lance:
I turned it in my hands; the stains
Of war were on it, and I wept,
Remembering how the Fenians stept
Along the blood-bedabbled plains,
Equal to good or grievous chance:
Thereon young Niamh softly came

And caught my hands, but spake no word
Save only many times my name,
In murmurs, like a frighted bird.
We passed by woods, and lawns of clover,
And found the horse and bridled him,
For we knew well the old was over.
I heard one say "His eyes grow dim
"With all the ancient sorrow of men";
And wrapped in dreams rode out again
With hoofs of the pale findrinny
Over the glimmering purple sea:
Under the golden evening light.
The immortals moved among the fountains
By rivers and the woods' old night;
Some danced like shadows on the mountains,
Some wandered ever hand in hand,
Or sat in dreams on the pale strand;
Each forehead like an obscure star
Bent down above each hooked knee:
And sang, and with a dreamy gaze
Watched where the sun in a saffron blaze
Was slumbering half in the sea ways;
And, as they sang, the painted birds
Kept time with their bright wings and feet;
Like drops of honey came their words,
But fainter than a young lamb's bleat.

"An old man stirs the fire to a blaze,
"In the house of a child, of a friend, of a brother
"He has over-lingered his welcome; the days,
"Grown desolate, whisper and sigh to each other;
"He hears the storm in the chimney above,
"And bends to the fire and shakes with the cold,
"While his heart still dreams of battle and love,
"And the cry of the hounds on the hills of old.

"But we are apart in the grassy places,
"Where care cannot trouble the least of our days,
"Or the softness of youth be gone from our faces,
"Or love's first tenderness die in our gaze.
"The hare grows old as she plays in the sun
"And gazes around her with eyes of brightness;
"Before the swift things that she dreamed of
     were done
"She limps along in an aged whiteness;
"A storm of birds in the Asian trees
"Like tulips in the air a-winging,
"And the gentle waves of the summer seas,
"That raise their heads and wander singing.
"Must murmur at last 'Unjust, unjust';
"And 'My speed is a weariness,' falters the mouse
"And the kingfisher turns to a ball of dust,
"And the roof falls in of his tunnelled house.

"But the love-dew dims our eyes till the day
"When God shall come from the sea with a sigh
"And bid the stars drop down from the sky,
"And the moon like a pale rose wither away."

Book II

Now, man of croziers, shadows called our names
And then away, away, like whirling flames;
And now fled by, mist-covered, without sound,
The youth and lady and the deer and hound;
"Gaze no more on the phantoms," Niamh said,
And kissed my eyes, and, swaying her bright head
And her bright body, sang of faery and man
Before God was or my old line began;
Wars shadowy, vast, exultant; faeries of old
Who wedded men with rings of Druid gold;
And how those lovers never turn their eyes
Upon the life that fades and flickers and dies,
But love and kiss on dim shores far away
Rolled round with music of the sighing spray:
But sang no more, as when, like a brown bee
That has drunk full, she crossed the misty sea
With me in her white arms a hundred years
Before this day; for now the fall of tears
Troubled her song.

I do not know if days
Or hours passed by, yet hold the morning rays
Shone many times among the glimmering flowers
Woven into her hair, before dark towers
Rose in the darkness, and the white surf gleamed
About them; and the horse of faery screamed
And shivered, knowing the Isle of many Fears,
Nor ceased until white Niamh stroked his ears
And named him by sweet names.

A foaming tide
Whitened afar with surge, fan-formed and wide,
Burst from a great door marred by many a blow
From mace and sword and pole-axe, long ago
When gods and giants warred. We rode between
The seaweed-covered pillars, and the green
And surging phosphorus alone gave light
On our dark pathway, till a countless flight
Of moonlit steps glimmered; and left and right
Dark statues glimmered over the pale tide
Upon dark thrones. Between the lids of one
The imaged meteors had flashed and run
And had disported in the stilly jet,
And the fixed stars had dawned and shone and set,
Since God made Time and Death and Sleep: the other
Stretched his long arm to where, a misty smother,
The stream churned, churned, and churned – his
    lips apart,

As though he told his never slumbering heart
Of every foamdrop on its misty way:
Tying the horse to his vast foot that lay
Half in the unvesselled sea, we climbed the stairs
And climbed so long, I thought the last steps were
Hung from the morning star; when these mild words
Fanned the delighted air like wings of birds:
"My brothers spring out of their beds at morn,
"A-murmur like young partridge: with loud horn
"They chase the noontide deer;
"And when the dew-drowned stars hang in the air
"Look to long fishing-lines, or point and pare
"An ash-wood hunting spear.

"O sigh, O fluttering sigh, be kind to me;
"Flutter along the froth lips of the sea,
"And shores, the froth lips wet:
"And stay a little while, and bid them weep:
"Ah, touch their blue-veined eyelids if they sleep,
"And shake their coverlet.

"When you have told how I weep endlessly,
"Flutter along the froth lips of the sea
"And home to me again,
"And in the shadow of my hair lie hid,
"And tell me how you came to one unbid,
"The saddest of all men."

A maiden with soft eyes like funeral tapers,
And face that seemed wrought out of moonlit vapours,
And a sad mouth, that fear made tremulous
As any ruddy moth, looked down on us;
And she with a wave-rusted chain was tied
To two old eagles, full of ancient pride,
That with dim eyeballs stood on either side.
Few feathers were on their dishevelled wings,
For their dim minds were with the ancient things.

"I bring deliverance," pearl-pale Niamh said.

"Neither the living, nor the unlabouring dead,
"Nor the high gods who never lived, may fight
"My enemy and hope; demons for fright
"Jabber and scream about him in the night;
"For he is strong and crafty as the seas
"That sprang under the Seven Hazel Trees,
"And I must needs endure and hate and weep,
"Until the gods and demons drop asleep,
"Hearing Aed touch the mournful strings of gold."

"Is he so dreadful?"

                              "Be not over bold,
"But flee while you may flee from him."

Then I:
"This demon shall be pierced and drop and die,
"And his loose bulk be thrown in the loud tide."

"Flee from him," pearl-pale Niamh weeping cried,
"For all men flee the demons"; but moved not
My angry, king remembering soul one jot;
There was no mightier soul of Heber's line;
Now it is old and mouse-like: for a sign
I burst the chain: still earless, nerveless, blind,
Wrapped in the things of the unhuman mind,
In some dim memory or ancient mood
Still earless, nerveless, blind, the eagles stood.

And then we climbed the stair to a high door;
A hundred horsemen on the basalt floor
Beneath had paced content: we held our way
And stood within: clothed in a misty ray
I saw a foam-white seagull drift and float
Under the roof, and with a straining throat
Shouted, and hailed him: he hung there a star,
For no man's cry shall ever mount so far;
Not even your God could have thrown down that hall;
Stabling His unloosed lightnings in their stall,
He had sat down and sighed with cumbered heart,
As though His hour were come.

                      We sought the part
That was most distant from the door; green slime

Made the way slippery, and time on time
Showed prints of sea-born scales, while down
      through it
The captive's journeys to and fro were writ
Like a small river, and, where feet touched, came
A momentary gleam of phosphorus flame.
Under the deepest shadows of the hall
That maiden found a ring hung on the wall,
And in the ring a torch, and with its flare
Making a world about her in the air,
Passed under a dim doorway, out of sight
And came again, holding a second light
Burning between her fingers, and in mine
Laid it and sighed: I held a sword whose shine
No centuries could dim: and a word ran
Thereon in Ogham letters, "Mananan";
That sea god's name, who in a deep content
Sprang dripping, and, with captive demons sent
Out of the seven-fold seas, built the dark hall
Rooted in foam and clouds, and cried to all
The mightier masters of a mightier race;
And at his cry there came no milk-pale face
Under a crown of thorns and dark with blood,
But only exultant faces.

                              Niamh stood
With bowed head, trembling when the white blade shone,
But she whose hours of tenderness were gone
Had neither hope nor fear. I bade them hide

Under the shadows till the tumults died
Of the loud crashing and earth shaking fight,
Lest they should look upon some dreadful sight;
And thrust the torch between the slimy flags.
A dome made out of endless carven jags,
Where shadowy face flowed into shadowy face,
Looked down on me; and in the self-same place
I waited hour by hour, and the high dome,
Windowless, pillarless, multitudinous home
Of faces, waited; and the leisured gaze
Was loaded with the memory of days
Buried and mighty. When through the great door
The dawn came in, and glimmered on the floor
With a pale light, I journeyed round the hall
And found a door deep sunken in the wall,
The least of doors; beyond on a dim plain
A little runnel made a bubbling strain,
And on the runnel's stony and bare edge
A husky demon dry as a withered sedge
Swayed, crooning to himself an unknown tongue:
In a sad revelry he sang and swung
Bacchant and mournful, passing to and fro
His hand along the runnel's side, as though
The flowers still grew there: far on the sea's waste
Shaking and waving, vapour vapour chased,
While high frail cloudlets, fed with a green light,
Like drifts of leaves, immovable and bright,
Hung in the passionate dawn. He slowly turned:

A demon's leisure: eyes, first white, now burned
Like wings of kingfishers; and he arose
Barking. We trampled up and down with blows
Of sword and brazen battle-axe, while day
Gave to high noon and noon to night gave way;
And when at withering of the sun he knew
The Druid sword of Mananan, he grew
To many shapes; I lunged at the smooth throat
Of a great eel; it changed, and I but smote
A fir-tree roaring in its leafless top;
I held a dripping corpse, with livid chop
And sunken shape, against my face and breast,
When I tore down the tree; but when the west
Surged up in plumy fire, I lunged and drave
Through heart and spine, and cast him in the wave,
Lest Niamh shudder.

                    Full of hope and dread
Those two came carrying wine and meat and bread,
And healed my wounds with unguents out of flowers
That feed white moths by some De Danaan shrine;
Then in that hall, lit by the dim sea shine,
We lay on skins of otters, and drank wine,
Brewed by the sea-gods, from huge cups that lay
Upon the lips of sea-gods in their day;
And then on heaped-up skins of otters slept.
But when the sun once more in saffron stept,
Rolling his flagrant wheel out of the deep,

We sang the loves and angers without sleep,
And all the exultant labours of the strong:

But now the lying clerics murder song
With barren words and flatteries of the weak.
In what land do the powerless turn the beak
Of ravening Sorrow, or the hand of Wrath?
For all your croziers, they have left the path
And wander in the storms and clinging snows,
Hopeless for ever: ancient Oisin knows,
For he is weak and poor and blind, and lies
On the anvil of the world.

S. PATRICK

               Be still: the skies
Are choked with thunder, lightning, and fierce wind,
For God has heard, and speaks His angry mind;
Go cast your body on the stones and pray,
For He has wrought midnight and dawn and day.

OISIN

Saint, do you weep? I hear amid the thunder
The Fenian horses; armour torn asunder;
Laughter and cries; the armies clash and shock;
All is done now; I see the ravens flock;
Ah, cease, you mournful, laughing Fenian horn!

We feasted for three days. On the fourth morn
I found, dropping sea foam on the wide stair,

And hung with slime, and whispering in his hair,
That demon dull and unsubduable;
And once more to a day-long battle fell,
And at the sundown threw him in the surge,
To lie until the fourth morn saw emerge
His new healed shape: and for a hundred years
So warred, so feasted, with nor dreams nor fears,
Nor languor nor fatigue: and endless feast,
An endless war.

               The hundred years had ceased;
I stood upon the stair: the surges bore
A beech bough to me, and my heart grew sore,
Remembering how I had stood by white-haired Finn
Under a beech at Emen and heard the thin
Outcry of bats.

               And then young Niamh came
Holding that horse, and sadly called my name;
I mounted, and we passed over the lone
And drifting grayness, while this monotone,
Surly and distant, mixed inseparably
Into the clangour of the wind and sea.

"I hear my soul drop down into decay,
"And Mananan's dark tower, stone by stone,
"Gather sea slime and fall the seaward way,
"And the moon goad the waters night and day,
"That all be overthrown.

"But till the moon has taken all, I wage
"War on the mightiest men under the skies,
"And they have fallen or fled, age after age:
"Light is man's love, and lighter is man's rage;
"His purpose drifts and dies."

And then lost Niamh murmured, "Love, we go
"To the Island of Forgetfulness, for lo!
"The Islands of Dancing and of Victories
"Are empty of all power."

     "And which of these
"Is the Island of Content?"

     "None know," she said;
And on my bosom laid her weeping head.

Book III

Fled foam underneath us, and around us, a wandering
 and milky smoke,
High as the saddle girth, covering away from our
 glances the tide;
And those that fled, and that followed, from the foam-
 pale distance broke;
The immortal desire of immortals we saw in their
 faces, and sighed.

I mused on the chase with the Fenians, and Bran,
    Sgeolan, Lomair,
And never a song sang Niamh, and over my finger-tips
Came now the sliding of tears and sweeping of mist-
    cold hair,
And now the warmth of sighs, and after the quiver
    of lips.

Were we days long or hours long in riding, when
    rolled in a grisly peace,
An isle lay level before us, with dripping hazel
    and oak?
And we stood on a sea's edge we saw not; for whiter
    than new-washed fleece
Fled foam underneath us, and round us, a wandering
    and milky smoke.

And we rode on the plains of the sea's edge; the sea's
    edge barren and gray,
Gray sand on the green of the grasses and over the
    dripping trees,
Dripping and doubling landward, as though they
    would hasten away
Like an army of old men longing for rest from the
    moan of the seas.

But the trees grew taller and closer, immense in their
    wrinkling bark;

Dropping; a murmurous dropping; old silence and
    that one sound;
For no live creatures lived there, no weasels moved in
    the dark:
Long sighs arose in our spirits, beneath us bubbled
    the ground.

And the ears of the horse went sinking away in the
    hollow night,
For, as drift from a sailor slow drowning the gleams of
    the world and the sun,
Ceased on our hands and our faces, on hazel and oak
    leaf, the light,
And the stars were blotted above us, and the whole of
    the world was one.

Till the horse gave a whinny; for, cumbrous with stems
    of the hazel and oak,
A valley flowed down from his hoofs, and there in the
    long grass lay,
Under the starlight and shadow, a monstrous
    slumbering folk,
Their naked and gleaming bodies poured out and
    heaped in the way.

And by them were arrow and war-axe, arrow and
    shield and blade;
And dew-blanched horns, in whose hollow a child of
    three years old

Could sleep on a couch of rushes, and all inwrought
    and inlaid,
And more comely than man can make them with
    bronze and silver and gold.

And each of the huge white creatures was huger than
    fourscore men;
The tops of their ears were feathered, their hands
    were the claws of birds,
And, shaking the plumes of the grasses and the leaves
    of the mural glen,
The breathing came from those bodies, long-warless,
    grown whiter than curds.

The wood was so spacious above them, that He who
    had stars for His flocks
Could fondle the leaves with His fingers, nor go from
    His dew-cumbered skies;
So long were they sleeping, the owls had builded their
    nests in their locks,
Filling the fibrous dimness with long generations
    of eyes.

And over the limbs and the valley the slow owls
    wandered and came,
Now in a place of star-fire, and now in a shadow
    place wide;
And the chief of the huge white creatures, his knees in
    the soft star-flame,

Lay loose in a place of shadow: we drew the reins by
    his side.

Golden the nails of his bird-claws, flung loosely along
    the dim ground;
In one was a branch soft-shining, with bells more
    many than sighs,
In midst of an old man's bosom; owls ruffling and
    pacing around,
Sidled their bodies against him, filling the shade with
    their eyes.

And my gaze was thronged with the sleepers; no, not
    since the world began,
In realms where the handsome were many, nor in
    glamours by demons flung,
Have faces alive with such beauty been known to the
    salt eye of man,
Yet weary with passions that faded when the seven-
    fold seas were young.

And I gazed on the bell-branch, sleep's forebear, far
    sung by the Sennachies.
I saw how those slumberers, grown weary, there
    camping in grasses deep,
Of wars with the wide world and pacing the shores of
    the wandering seas,
Laid hands on the bell-branch and swayed it, and fed
    of unhuman sleep.

Snatching the horn of Niamh, I blew a lingering note;
Came sound from those monstrous sleepers, a sound
  like the stirring of flies.
He, shaking the fold of his lips, and heaving the pillar
  of his throat,
Watched me with mournful wonder out of the wells
  of his eyes.

I cried, "Come out of the shadow, king of the nails
  of gold!
"And tell of your goodly household and the goodly
  works of your hands,
"That we may muse in the starlight and talk of the
  battles of old;
"Your questioner, Oisin, is worthy, he comes from the
  Fenian lands."

Half open his eyes were, and held me, dull with the
  smoke of their dreams;
His lips moved slowly in answer, no answer out of
  them came;
Then he swayed in his fingers the bell-branch, slow
  dropping a sound in faint streams
Softer than snow-flakes in April and piercing the
  marrow like flame.

Wrapt in the wave of that music, with weariness more
  than of earth,

The moil of my centuries filled me; and gone like a
    sea-covered stone
Were the memories of the whole of my sorrow and
    the memories of the whole of my mirth,
And a softness came from the starlight and filled me
    full to the bone.

In the roots of the grasses, the sorrels, I laid my body
    as low;
And the pearl-pale Niamh lay by me, her brow on the
    midst of my breast;
And the horse was gone in the distance, and years
    after years 'gan flow;
Square leaves of the ivy moved over us, binding us
    down to our rest.

And, man of the many white croziers, a century there
    I forgot;
How the fetlocks drip blood in the battle, when the
    fallen on fallen lie rolled;
How the falconer follows the falcon in the weeds of
    the heron's plot,
And the names of the demons whose hammers made
    armour for Conhor of old.

And, man of the many white croziers, a century there
    I forgot;
That the spear-shaft is made out of ashwood, the
    shield out of ozier and hide;

How the hammers spring on the anvil, on the
     spearhead's burning spot;
How the slow, blue-eyed oxen of Finn low sadly at
     evening tide.

But in dreams, mild man of the croziers, driving the
     dust with their throngs,
Moved round me, of seamen or landsmen, all who are
     winter tales;
Came by me the kings of the Red Branch, with roaring
     of laughter and songs,
Or moved as they moved once, love-making or
     piercing the tempest with sails.

Came Blanid, Mac Nessa, tall Fergus who feastward of
     old time slunk,
Cook Barach, the traitor; and warward, the spittle on
     his beard never dry,
Dark Balor, as old as a forest, car borne, his mighty
     head sunk
Helpless, men lifting the lids of his weary and death-
     making eye.

And by me, in soft red raiment, the Fenians moved in
     loud streams,
And Grania, walking and smiling, sewed with her
     needle of bone,
So lived I and lived not, so wrought I and wrought not,
     with creatures of dreams,

In a long iron sleep, as a fish in the water goes dumb
   as a stone.

At times our slumber was lightened. When the sun
   was on silver or gold;
When brushed with the wings of the owls, in the
   dimness they love going by;
When a glow-worm was green on a grass leaf, lured
   from his lair in the mould;
Half wakening, we lifted our eyelids, and gazed on the
   grass with a sigh.

So watched I when, man of the croziers, at the heel of
   a century fell,
Weak, in the midst of the meadow, from his miles in
   the midst of the air,
A starling like them that forgathered 'neath a moon
   waking white as a shell.
When the Fenians made foray at morning with Bran,
   Sgeolan, Lomair.

I awoke: the strange horse without summons out of
   the distance ran,
Thrusting his nose to my shoulder; he knew in his
   bosom deep
That once more moved in my bosom the ancient
   sadness of man,
And that I would leave the immortals, their dimness,
   their dews dropping sleep.

O, had you seen beautiful Niamh grow white as the
    waters are white,
Lord of the croziers, you even had lifted your hands
    and wept:
But, the bird in my fingers, I mounted, remembering
    alone that delight
Of twilight and slumber were gone, and that hoofs
    impatiently stept.

I cried, "O Niamh! O white one! if only a twelve-
    houred day,
"I must gaze on the beard of Finn, and move where
    the old men and young
"In the Fenians' dwellings of wattle lean on the
    chessboards and play,
"Ah, sweet to me now were even bald Conan's
    slanderous tongue!

"Like me were some galley forsaken far off in
    Meridian isle.
"Remembering its long-oared companions, sails
    turning to thread-bare rags;
"No more to crawl on the seas with long oars mile
    after mile,
"But to be amid shooting of flies and flowering of
    rushes and flags."

Their motionless eyeballs of spirits grown mild with
    mysterious thought

Watched her those seamless faces from the valley's
    glimmering girth;
As she murmured, "O wandering Oisin, the strength of
    the bell-branch is naught,
"For there moves alive in your fingers the fluttering
    sadness of earth.

"Then go through the lands in the saddle and see
    what the mortals do,
"And softly come to your Niamh over the tops of
    the tide;
"But weep for your Niamh, O Oisin, weep; for if only
    your shoe
"Brush lightly as haymouse earth's pebbles, you will
    come no more to my side.

"O flaming lion of the world, O when will you turn to
    your rest?"
"I saw from a distant saddle; from the earth she made
    her moan;
"I would die like a small withered leaf in the autumn,
    for breast unto breast
"We shall mingle no more, nor our gazes empty their
    sweetness lone.

"In the isles of the farthest seas where only the
    spirits come.
"Were the winds less soft than the breath of a pigeon
    who sleeps on her nest,

"Nor lost in the star-fires and odours the sound of the
        sea's vague drum?
"O flaming lion of the world, O when will you turn to
        your rest?"

The wailing grew distant; I rode by the woods of the
        wrinkling bark,
Where ever is murmurous dropping, old silence and
        that one sound;
For no live creatures live there, no weasels move in
        the dark;
In a reverie forgetful of all things, over the
        bubbling ground.

And I rode by the plains of the sea's edge, where all is
        barren and gray,
Gray sands on the green of the grasses and over the
        dripping trees,
Dripping and doubling landward, as though they
        would hasten away,
Like an army of old men lounging for rest from the
        moan of the seas.

And the winds made the sands on the sea's edge
        turning and turning go,
As my mind made the names of the Fenians. Far from
        the hazel and oak,
I rode away on the surges, where, high as the
        saddle bow,

Fled foam underneath me, and round me, a
   wandering and milky smoke.

Long fled the foam-flakes around me, the winds fled
   out of the vast,
Snatching the bird in secret; nor knew I,
   embosomed apart,
When they froze the cloth on my body like armour
   riveted fast,
For Remembrance, lifting her leanness, keened in the
   gates of my heart.

Till fattening the winds of the morning, an odour of
   new-mown hay
Came, and my forehead fell low, and my tears like
   berries fell down;
Later a sound came, half lost in the sound of a shore
   far away,
From the great grass-barnacle calling, and later the
   shore-weeds brown.

If I were as I once was, the strong hoofs crushing the
   sand and the shells,
Coming out of the sea as the dawn comes, a chaunt of
   love on my lips,
Not coughing, my head on my knees, and praying, and
   wroth with the bells,
I would leave no saint's head on his body from Rachlin
   to Bera of ships.

Making way from the kindling surges, I rode on
    a bridle-path
Much wondering to see upon all hands, of wattles and
    woodwork made,
Your bell-mounted churches, and guardless the sacred
    cairn and the rath,
And a small and a feeble populace stooping with
    mattock and spade.

Or weeding or ploughing with faces a-shining with
    much-toil wet;
While in this place and that place, with bodies
    unglorious, their chieftains stood,
Awaiting in patience the straw-death, croziered one,
    caught in your net:
Went the laughter of scorn from my mouth like the
    roaring of wind in a wood.

And because I went by them so huge and so speedy
    with eyes so bright,
Came after the hard gaze of youth, or an old man
    lifted his head:
And I rode and I rode, and I cried out, "The Fenians
    hunt wolves in the night,
So sleep thee by daytime." A voice cried, "The Fenians
    a long time are dead."

A whitebeard stood hushed on the pathway, the flesh
    of his face as dried grass,

And in folds round his eyes and his mouth, he sad as a
    child without milk;
And the dreams of the islands were gone, and I knew
    how men sorrow and pass,
And their hound, and their horse, and their love, and
    their eyes that glimmer like silk.

And wrapping my face in my hair, I murmured, "In old
    age they ceased";
And my tears were larger than berries, and I
    murmured, "Where white clouds lie spread
"On Crevroe or broad Knockfefin, with many of old
    they feast
"On the floors of the gods." He cried, "No, the gods a
    long time are dead."

And lonely and longing for Niamh, I shivered and
    turned me about,
The heart in me longing to leap like a grasshopper
    into her heart;
I turned and rode to the westward, and followed the
    sea's old shout
Till I saw where Maeve lies sleeping till starlight and
    midnight part.

And there at the foot of the mountain, two carried a
    sack full of sand,
They bore it with staggering and sweating, but fell with
    their burden at length:

Leaning down from the gem-studded saddle, I flung it
    five yards with my hand,
With a sob for men waxing so weakly, a sob for the
    Fenian's old strength.

The rest you have heard of, O croziered one; how,
    when divided the girth,
I fell on the path, and the horse went away like a
    summer fly;
And my years three hundred fell on me, and I rose,
    and walked on the earth,
A creeping old man, full of sleep, with the spittle on
    his beard never dry.

How the men of the sand-sack showed me a church
    with its belfry in air;
Sorry place, where for swing of the war-axe in my dim
    eyes the crozier gleams;
What place have Caolte and Conan, and Bran,
    Sgeolan, Lomair?
Speak, you too are old with your memories, an old
    man surrounded with dreams.

S. PATRICK
Where the flesh of the footsole clingeth on the
    burning stones is their place;
Where the demons whip them with wires on the
    burning stones of wide hell,

Watching the blessed ones move far off, and the smile
 on God's face,
Between them a gateway of brass, and the howl of the
 angels who fell.

OISIN
Put the staff in my hands; for I go to the Fenians, O
 cleric, to chaunt
The war-songs that roused them of old; they will rise,
 making clouds with their breath
Innumerable, singing, exultant; the clay underneath
 them shall pant,
And demons be broken in pieces, and trampled
 beneath them in death.

And demons afraid in their darkness; deep horror of
 eyes and of wings,
Afraid their ears on the earth laid, shall listen and rise
 up and weep;
Hearing the shaking of shields and the quiver of
 stretched bowstrings,
Hearing hell loud with a murmur, as shouting and
 mocking we sweep.

We will tear out the flaming stones, and batter the
 gateway of brass
And enter, and none sayeth "No" when there enters
 the strongly armed guest;

Make clean as a broom cleans, and march on as oxen
    move over young grass;
Then feast, making converse of wars, and of old
    wounds, and turn to our rest.

S. PATRICK
On the flaming stones, without refuge, the limbs of
    the Fenians are tost;
None war on the masters of Hell, who could break up
    the world in their rage;
But kneel and wear out the flags and pray for your
    soul that is lost
Through the demon love of its youth and its godless
    and passionate age.

OISIN
Ah, me! to be shaken with coughing and broken with
    old age and pain,
Without laughter, a show unto children, alone with
    remembrance and fear;
All emptied of purple hours as a beggar's cloak in
    the rain,
As a hay-cock out on the flood, or a wolf sucked under
    a weir.

It were sad to gaze on the blessed and no man I loved
    of old there;
I throw down the chain of small stones! when life in
    my body has ceased,

I will go to Caolte, and Conan, and Bran,
    Sgeolan, Lomair,
And dwell in the house of the Fenians, be they in
    flames or at feast.

TO THE ROSE UPON THE ROOD OF TIME

Red Rose, proud Rose, sad Rose of all my days!
Come near me, while I sing the ancient ways:
Cuchulain battling with the bitter tide;
The Druid, gray, wood-nurtured, quiet-eyed,
Who cast round Fergus dreams, and ruin untold;
And thine own sadness, whereof stars, grown old
In dancing silver sandalled on the sea,
Sing in their high and lonely melody.
Come near, that no more blinded by man's fate,
I find under the boughs of love and hate,
In all poor foolish things that live a day,
Eternal beauty wandering on her way.

Come near, come near, come near – Ah, leave me still
A little space for the rose-breath to fill!
Lest I no more hear common things that crave;
The weak worm hiding down in its small cave,
The field mouse running by me in the grass,
And heavy mortal hopes that toil and pass;
But seek alone to hear the strange things said
By God to the bright hearts of those long dead,
And learn to chaunt a tongue men do not know.
Come near; I would, before my time to go,
Sing of old Eire and the ancient ways:
Red Rose, proud Rose, sad Rose of all my days.

FERGUS AND THE DRUID

FERGUS
The whole day have I followed in the rocks,
And you have changed and flowed from shape
    to shape.
First as a raven on whose ancient wings
Scarcely a feather lingered, then you seemed
A weasel moving on from stone to stone,
And now at last you wear a human shape,
A thin gray man half lost in gathering night.

DRUID
What would you, king of the proud Red Branch kings?

FERGUS
This would I say, most wise of living souls:
Young subtle Concobar sat close by me
When I gave judgment, and his words were wise,
And what to me was burden without end,
To him seemed easy, so I laid the crown
Upon his head to cast away my care.

DRUID
What would you, king of the proud Red Branch kings?

FERGUS
I feast amid my people on the hill,

And pace the woods, and drive my chariot wheels
In the white border of the murmuring sea;
And still I feel the crown upon my head.

DRUID
What would you?

FERGUS
                  I would be no more a king
But learn the dreaming wisdom that is yours.

DRUID
Look on my thin gray hair and hollow cheeks
And on these hands that may not lift the sword
This body trembling like a wind-blown reed.
No woman loves me, no man seeks my help,
Because I be not of the things I dream.

FERGUS
A wild and foolish labourer is a king,
To do and do and do, and never dream.

DRUID
Take, if you must, this little bag of dreams;
Unloose the cord, and they will wrap you round.

FERGUS
I see my life go dripping like a stream

From change to change; I have been many things,
A green drop in the surge, a gleam of light
Upon a sword, a fir-tree on a hill,
An old slave grinding at a heavy quern,
A king sitting upon a chair of gold,
And all these things were wonderful and great;
But now I have grown nothing, being all,
And the whole world weighs down upon my heart:
Ah! Druid, Druid, how great webs of sorrow
Lay hidden in the small slate-coloured bag!

THE DEATH OF CUCHULAIN

A man came slowly from the setting sun,
To Forgail's daughter, Emer, in her dun,
And found her dyeing cloth with subtle care,
And said, casting aside his draggled hair:
"I am Aleel, the swineherd, whom you bid
"Go dwell upon the sea cliffs, vapour hid;
"But now my years of watching are no more."

Then Emer cast the web upon the floor,
And stretching out her arms, red with the dye,
Parted her lips with a loud sudden cry.

Looking on her, Aleel, the swineherd, said:
"Not any god alive, nor mortal dead,
"Has slain so mighty armies, so great kings,
"Nor won the gold that now Cuchulain brings."

"Why do you tremble thus from feet to crown?"

Aleel, the swineherd, wept and cast him down
Upon the web-heaped floor, and thus his word:
"With him is one sweet-throated like a bird."

"Who bade you tell these things?" and then she cried
To those about, "Beat him with thongs of hide
"And drive him from the door."

                    And thus it was:
And where her son, Finmole, on the smooth grass
Was driving cattle, came she with swift feet,
And called out to him, "Son, it is not meet
"That you stay idling here with flocks and herds."

"I have long waited, mother, for those words:
"But wherefore now?"

                    "There is a man to die;
"You have the heaviest arm under the sky."

"My father dwells among the sea-worn bands,
"And breaks the ridge of battle with his hands."

"Nay, you are taller than Cuchulain, son."

"He is the mightiest man in ship or dun."

"Nay, he is old and sad with many wars,
"And weary of the crash of battle cars."

"I only ask what way my journey lies,
"For God, who made you bitter, made you wise."

"The Red Branch kings a tireless banquet keep,
"Where the sun falls into the Western deep.
"Go there, and dwell on the green forest rim;

"But tell alone your name and house to him
"Whose blade compels, and bid them send you one
"Who has a like vow from their triple dun."

Between the lavish shelter of a wood
And the gray tide, the Red Branch multitude
Feasted, and with them old Cuchulain dwelt,
And his young dear one close beside him knelt,
And gazed upon the wisdom of his eyes,
More mournful than the depth of starry skies,
And pondered on the wonder of his days;
And all around the harp-string told his praise,
And Concobar, the Red Branch king of kings,
With his own fingers touched the brazen strings.
At last Cuchulain spake, "A young man strays
"Driving the deer along the woody ways.
"I often hear him singing to and fro,
"I often hear the sweet sound of his bow,
"Seek out what man he is."

                         One went and came.
"He bade me let all know he gives his name
"At the sword point, and bade me bring him one
"Who had a like vow from our triple dun."

"I only of the Red Branch hosted now,"
Cuchulain cried, "have made and keep that vow."

After short fighting in the leafy shade,
He spake to the young man, "Is there no maid
"Who loves you, no white arms to wrap you round,
"Or do you long for the dim sleepy ground,
"That you come here to meet this ancient sword?"

"The dooms of men are in God's hidden hoard."

"Your head a while seemed like a woman's head
"That I loved once."

                Again the fighting sped,
But now the war rage in Cuchulain woke,
And through the other's shield his long blade broke,
And pierced him.

                "Speak before your breath is done."
"I am Finmole, mighty Cuchulain's son."

"I put you from your pain. I can no more."

While day its burden on to evening bore,
With head bowed on his knees Cuchulain stayed;
Then Concobar sent that sweet-throated maid,
And she, to win him, his gray hair caressed;
In vain her arms, in vain her soft white breast.
Then Concobar, the subtlest of all men,
Ranking his Druids round him ten by ten,

Spake thus, "Cuchulain will dwell there and brood,
"For three days more in dreadful quietude,
"And then arise, and raving slay us all.
"Go, cast on him delusions magical,
"That he might fight the waves of the loud sea."
And ten by ten under a quicken tree,
The Druids chaunted, swaying in their hands
Tall wands of alder, and white quicken wands.

In three days' time, Cuchulain with a moan
Stood up, and came to the long sands alone:
For four days warred he with the bitter tide;
And the waves flowed above him, and he died.

A FAERY SONG

Sung by the people of faery over Diarmuid and Grania, who lay in their bridal sleep under a Cromlech.

We who are old, old and gay,
O so old!
Thousands of years, thousands of years,
If all were told:

Give to these children, new from the world,
Silence and love;
And the long dew-dropping hours of the night,
And the stars above:

Give to these children, new from the world,
Rest far from men.
Is anything better, anything better?
Tell us it then:

Us who are old, old and gay,
O so old!
Thousands of years, thousands of years,
If all were told.

WHO GOES WITH FERGUS?

Who will go drive with Fergus now,
And pierce the deep wood's woven shade,
And dance upon the level shore?
Young man, lift up your russet brow,
And lift your tender eyelids, maid,
And brood on hopes and fears no more.

And no more turn aside and brood
Upon Love's bitter mystery;
For Fergus rules the brazen cars,
And rules the shadows of the wood,
And the white breast of the dim sea
And all dishevelled wandering stars.

A DREAM OF A BLESSED SPIRIT

All the heavy days are over;
Leave the body's coloured pride
Underneath the grass and clover,
With the feet laid side by side.

One with her are mirth and duty,
Bear the gold embroidered dress,
For she needs not her sad beauty,
To the scented oaken press.

Hers the kiss of Mother Mary,
The long hair is on her face;
Still she goes with footsteps wary,
Full of earth's old timid grace.

With white feet of angels seven
Her white feet go glimmering
And above the deep of heaven,
Flame on flame and wing on wing.

THE MAN WHO DREAMED
OF FAERYLAND

He stood among a crowd at Drumahair;
His heart hung all upon a silken dress,
And he had known at last some tenderness,
Before earth made of him her sleepy care;
But when a man poured fish into a pile,
It seemed they raised their little silver heads,
And sang how day a Druid twilight sheds
Upon a dim, green, well-beloved isle,
Where people love beside star-laden seas;
How Time may never mar their faery vows
Under the woven roofs of quicken boughs:
The singing shook him out of his new ease.

He wandered by the sands of Lisadill;
His mind ran all on money cares and fears,
And he had known at last some prudent years
Before they heaped his grave under the hill;
But while he passed before a plashy place,
A lug-worm with its gray and muddy mouth
Sang how somewhere to north or west or south
There dwelt a gay, exulting, gentle race;
And how beneath those three times blessed skies
A Danaan fruitage makes a shower of moons,
And as it falls awakens leafy tunes:
And at that singing he was no more wise.

He mused beside the well of Scanavin,
He mused upon his mockers: without fail
His sudden vengeance were a country tale,
Now that deep earth has drunk his body in;
But one small knot-grass growing by the pool
Told where, ah, little, all-unneeded voice!
Old Silence bids a lonely folk rejoice,
And chaplet their calm brows with leafage cool,
And how, when fades the sea-strewn rose of day,
A gentle feeling wraps them like a fleece,
And all their trouble dies into its peace:
The tale drove his fine angry mood away.

He slept under the hill of Lugnagall;
And might have known at last unhaunted sleep
Under that cold and vapour-turbaned steep,
Now that old earth had taken man and all:
Were not the worms that spired about his bones
A-telling with their low and reedy cry,
Of how God leans His hands out of the sky,
To bless that isle with honey in His tones;
That none may feel the power of squall and wave
And no one any leaf-crowned dancer miss
Until He burn up Nature with a kiss:
The man has found no comfort in the grave.

THE HOSTING OF THE SIDHE

The host is riding from Knocknarea
And over the grave of Clooth-na-bare;
Caolte tossing his burning hair
And Niamh calling *Away, come away:*
Empty your heart of its mortal dream.
The winds awaken, the leaves while round,
Our cheeks are pale, our hair is unbound,
Our breasts are heaving, our eyes are a-glean,
Our arms are waving, our lips are apart;
And if any gaze on our rushing band,
We come between him and the deed of this hand,
We come between him and the hope of his heart.
The host is rushing 'twixt night and day,
And where is there hope or deed as fair?
Caolte tossing his burning hair,
And Niamh calling *Away, come away.*

THE EVERLASTING VOICES

O sweet everlasting Voices be still;
Go to the guards of the heavenly fold
And bid them wander obeying your will
Flame under flame, till Time be no more;
Have you not heard that our hearts are old,
That you call in birds, in wind on the hill,
In shaken boughs, in tide on the shore?
O sweet everlasting Voices be still.

A CRADLE SONG

The Danann children laugh, in cradles of
   wrought gold,
And clap their hands together, and half close
   their eyes,
For they will ride the North when the ger-eagle flies,
With heavy whitening wings, and a heart fallen cold:
I kiss my wailing child and press it to my breast,
And hear the narrow graves calling my child and me.
Desolate winds that cry over the wandering sea;
Desolate winds that hover in the flaming West;
Desolate winds that beat the doors of Heaven, and beat
The doors of Hell and blow there many a
   whimpering ghost;
O heart the winds have shaken; the unappeasable host
Is comelier than candles at Maurya's feet.

THE SONG OF WANDERING AENGUS

I went out to the hazel wood,
Because a fire was in my head,
And cut and peeled a hazel wand,
And hooked a berry to a thread;
And when white moths were on the wing,
And moth-like stars were flickering out,
I dropped the berry in a steam
And caught a little silver trout.

When I had laid it on the floor
I went to blow the fire a-flame,
But something rustled on the floor,
And someone called me by my name:
It had become a glimmering girl
With apple blossom in her hair
Who called me by my name and ran
And faded through the brightening air.

Though I am old with wandering
Through hollow lands and hilly lands,
I will find out where she has gone,
And kiss her lips and take her hands;
And walk among long dappled grass,
And pluck till time and times are done,
The silver apples of the moon,
The golden apples of the sun.

MONGAN LAMENTS THE CHANGE
THAT HAS COME UPON HIM AND
HIS BELOVED

Do you not hear me calling, white deer with no horns!
I have been changed to a hound with one red ear;
I have been in the Path of Stones and the Wood
    of Thorns.
For somebody hid hatred and hope and desire
    and fear
Under my feet that they follow you night and day.
A man with a hazel wand came without sound;
He changed me suddenly; I was looking an other way;
And now my calling is but the calling of a hound;
And Time and Birth and Change are hurrying by.
I would that the boar without bristles had come from
    the West
And had rooted the sun and moon and stars out of
    the sky
And lay in the darkness, grunting, and turning to
    his rest.

THE BLESSED

Cumhal called out, bending his head,
Till Dathi came and stood,
With a blink in his eyes at the cave mouth,
Between the wind and the wood.

And Cumhal said, bending his knees,
"I have come by the windy way
"To gather the half of your blessedness
"And learn to pray when you pray.

"I can bring you salmon out of the streams
"And heron cut of the skies."
But Dathi folded his hands and smiled
With the secrets of God in his eyes.

And Cumhal saw like a drifting smoke
All manner of blessed souls,
Women and children, young men with books,
And old men with croziers and stoles,

"Praise God and God's mother," Dathi said,
For God and God's mother have sent
"The blessedest souls that walk in the world
"To fill your heart with content,"

"And which is the blessedest," Cumhal said,
"Where all are comely and good?
"Is it these that with golden thuribles
"Are singing about the wood?"

"My eyes are blinking," Dathi said,
"With the secrets of God half blind,
"But I can see where the wind goes
"And follow the way of the wind;

"And blessedness goes where the wind goes,
"And when it is gone we are dead;
"I see the blessedest soul in the world
"And he nods a drunken head.

"O blessedness comes in the night and the day
"And whither the wise heart knows;
"And one has seen in the redness of wine
"The Incorruptible Rose,

"That drowsily drops faint leaves on him
"And the sweetness of desire,
"While time and the world are ebbing away
"In twilights of dew and of fire."

MONGAN THINKS OF HIS
PAST GREATNESS

I have drunk ale from the Country of the Young
And weep because I know all things now:
I have been a hazel tree and they hung
The Pilot Star and the Crooked Plough
Among my leaves in times out of mind:
I became a rush that horses tread:
I became a man, a hater of the wind,
Knowing one, out of all things, alone, that his head
Would not lie on the breast or his lips on the hair
Of the woman that he loves, until he dies;
Although the rushes and the fowl of the air
Cry of his love with their pitiful cries.

THE OLD AGE OF QUEEN MAEVE

Maeve the great queen was pacing to and fro,
Between the walls covered with beaten bronze,
In her high house at Cruachan; the long hearth,
Flickering with ash and hazel, but half showed
Where the tired horse-boys lay upon the rushes,
Or on the benches underneath the walls,
In comfortable sleep; all living slept
But that great queen, who more than half the night
Had paced from door to fire and fire to door.
Though now in her old age, in her young age
She had been beautiful in that old way
That's all but gone; for the proud heart is gone
And the fool heart of the counting-house fears all
But soft beauty and indolent desire.
She could have called over the rim of the world
Whatever woman's lover had hit her fancy,
And yet had been great bodied and great limbed,
Fashioned to be the mother of strong children;
And she'd had lucky eyes and a high heart,
And wisdom that caught fire like the dried flax,
At need, and made her beautiful and fierce,
Sudden and laughing.
            O unquiet heart,
Why do you praise another, praising her,
As if there were no tale but your own tale
Worth knitting to a measure of sweet sound?.

Have I not bid you tell of that great queen
Who has been buried some two thousand years?.

When night was at its deepest, a wild goose
Cried from the porter's lodge, and with long clamour
Shook the ale horns and shields upon their hooks;
But the horse-boys slept on, as though some power
Had filled the house with Druid heaviness;
And wondering who of the many changing Sidhe
Had come as in the old times to counsel her,
Maeve walked, yet with slow footfall being old,
To that small chamber by the outer gate.
The porter slept although he sat upright
With still and stony limbs and open eyes.
Maeve waited, and when that ear-piercing noise
Broke from his parted lips and broke again,
She laid a hand on either of his shoulders,
And shook him wide awake, and bid him say
Who of the wandering many-changing ones
Had troubled his sleep. But all he had to say
Was that, the air being heavy and the dogs
More still than they had been for a good month,
He had fallen asleep, and, though he had
    dreamed nothing,
He could remember when he had had fine dreams.
It was before the time of the great war
Over the White-Horned Bull, and the Brown Bull.

She turned away; he turned again to sleep
That no god troubled now, and, wondering
What matters were afoot among the Sidhe,
Maeve walked through that great hall, and with a sigh
Lifted the curtain of her sleeping room,
Remembering that she too had seemed divine
To many thousand eyes, and to her own
One that the generations had long waited
That work too difficult for mortal hands
Might be accomplished. Bunching the curtain up
She saw her husband Ailell sleeping there,
And thought of days when he'd had a straight body,
And of that famous Fergus, Nessa's husband,
Who had been the lover of her middle life.

Suddenly Ailell spoke out of his sleep,
And not with his own voice or a man's voice,
But with the burning, live, unshaken voice
Of those that it may be can never age.
He said "High Queen of Cruachan and Mag Ai
A king of the Great Plain would speak with you."
And with glad voice Maeve answered him "What King
Of the far wandering shadows has come to me?
As in the old days when they would come and go
About my threshold to counsel and to help."
The parted lips replied "I seek your help,
For I am Aengus and I am crossed in love."

"How may a mortal whose life gutters out
Help them that wander with hand clasping hand
By rivers where nor rain nor hail has dimmed
Their haughty images, that cannot fade
Although their beauty's like a hollow dream"

"I come from the undimmed rivers to bid you call
The children of the Maines out of sleep,
And set them digging into Anbual's hill.
We shadows, while they uproot his earthy house,
Will overthrow his shadows and carry off
Caer, his blue eyed daughter that I love.
I helped your fathers when they built these walls
And I would have your help in my great need,
Queen of high Cruachan".
                              "I obey your will
With speedy feet and a most thankful heart:
For you have been, O Aengus of the birds
Our giver of good counsel and good luck".
And with a groan, as if the mortal breath
Could but awaken sadly upon lips
That happier breath had moved, her husband turned
Face downward, tossing in a troubled sleep;
But Maeve, and not with a slow feeble foot,
Came to the threshold of the painted house,
Where her grandchildren slept, and cried aloud,
Until the pillared dark began to stir
With shouting and the clang of unhooked arms.

She told them of the many-changing ones;
And all that night, and all through the next day
To middle night, they dug into the hill.
At middle night great cats with silver claws,
Bodies of shadow and blind eyes like pearls,
Came up out of the hole, and red-eared hounds
With long white bodies came out of the air
Suddenly, and ran at them and harried them.

The Maines' children dropped their spades, and stood
With quaking joints and terror strucken faces,
Till Maeve called out "These are but common men.
The Maines' children have not dropped their spades
Because Earth crazy for its broken power
Casts up a show and the winds answer it
With holy shadows". Her high heart was glad,
And when the uproar ran along the grass
She followed with light footfall in the midst,
Till it died out where an old thorn tree stood.

Friend of these many years, you too had stood
With equal courage in that whirling rout;
For you, although you've not her wandering heart,
Have all that greatness, and not hers alone.
For there is no high story about queens
In any ancient book but tells of you,
And when I've heard how they grew old and died
Or fell into unhappiness I've said;

"She will grow old and die and she has wept"!
And when I'd write it out anew, the words,
Half crazy with the thought, She too has wept!
Outrun the measure.
                  I'd tell of that great queen
Who stood amid a silence by the thorn
Until two lovers came out of the air
With bodies made out of soft fire. The one
About whose face birds wagged their fiery wings
Said, "Aengus and his sweetheart give their thanks
To Maeve and to Maeve's household, owing all
In owing them the bride-bed that gives peace".
Then Maeve, "O Aengus, Master of all lovers,
A thousand years ago you held high talk
With the first kings of many pillared Cruachan
O when will you grow weary".
                They had vanished,
But out of the dark air over her head there came
A murmur of soft words and meeting lips.

BAILE AND AILLINN

Argument. Baile and Aillinn were lovers, but Aengus, the
Master of Love, wishing them to be happy in his own
land among the dead, told to each a story of the others
death, so that their hearts were broken and they died.

I hardly hear the curlew cry,
Nor the grey rush when wind is high,
Before my thoughts begin to run
On the heir of Ulad, Buan's son,
Baile who had the honey mouth,
And that mild woman of the south,
Aillinn, who was King Lugaid's heir.
Their love was never drowned in care
Of this or that thing, nor grew cold
Because their bodies had grown old;
Being forbid to marry on earth
They blossomed to immortal mirth.

About the time when Christ was born,
When the long wars for the White Horn
And the Brown Bull had not yet come,
Young Baile Honey-Mouth, whom some
Called rather Baile Little-Land,
Rode out of Emain with a band
Of harpers and young men, and they
Imagined, as they struck the way
To many pastured Muirthemne,
That all things fell out happily

And there,for all that fools had said,
Baile and Aillinn would be wed.

They found an old man running there,
He had ragged long grass-yellow hair;
He had knees that stuck out of his hose;
He had puddle water in his shoes;
He had half a cloak to keep him dry;
Although he had a squirrel's eye.

O wandering birds and rushy beds
You put such folly in our heads
With all this crying in the wind
No common love is to our mind,
And our poor Kate or Nan is less
Than any whose unhappiness
Awoke the harp strings long ago.
Yet they that know all things but know
That all life had to give us is
A child's laughter, a woman's kiss.
Who was it put so great a scorn
In the grey reeds that night and morn
Are trodden and broken by the herds,
And in the light bodies of birds
That north wind tumbles to and fro
And pinches among hail and snow?

That runner said "I am from the south;
I run to Baile Honey-Mouth

To tell him how the girl Aillinn
Rode from the country of her kin
And old and young men rode with her:
For all that country had been astir
If anybody half as fair
Had chosen a husband anywhere
But where it could see her every day.
When they had ridden a little way
An old man caught the horse's head
With 'You must home again and wed
With somebody in your own land'.
A young man cried and kissed her hand
'O lady, wed with one of us;'
And when no face grew piteous
For any gentle thing she spake
She fell and died of the heart-break".

Because a lover's heart's worn out
Being tumbled and blown about
By its own blind imagining,
And will believe that anything
That is bad enough to be true, is true,
Baile's heart was broken in two;
And he being laid upon green boughs
Was carried to the goodly house
Where the Hound of Ulad sat before
The brazen pillars of his door;
His face bowed low to weep the end
Of the harper's daughter and her friend;

For although years had passed away
He always wept them on that day,
For on that day they had been betrayed;
And now that Honey-Mouth is laid
Under a cairn of sleepy stone
Before his eyes, he has tears for none,
Although he is carrying stone, but two
For whom the cairn's but heaped anew.

We hold because our memory is
So full of that thing and of this
That out of sight is out of mind.
But the grey rush under the wind
And the grey bird with crooked bill
Have such long memories that they still
Remember Deirdre and her man,
And when we walk with Kate or Nan
About the windy water side
Our heart can hear the voices chide.
How could we be so soon content
Who know the way that Naoise went?
And they have news of Deirdre's eyes
Who being lovely was so wise
Ah wise, my heart knows well how wise.

Now had that old gaunt crafty one,
Gathering his cloak about him, run
Where Aillinn rode with waiting maids

Who amid leafy lights and shades
Dreamed of the hands that would unlace
Their bodices in some dim place
When they had come to the marriage bed;
And harpers pondering with bowed head
A music that had thought enough
Of the ebb of all things to make love
Grow gentle without sorrowings;
And leather-coated men with slings
Who peered about on every side;
And amid leafy light he cried,
"He is well out of wind and wave,
They have heaped the stones above his grave
In Muirthemne and over it
In changeless Ogham letters writ
Baile that was of Rury's seed.
But the gods long ago decreed
No waiting maid should ever spread
Baile and Aillinn's marriage bed,
For they should clip and clip again
Where wild bees hive on the Great Plain.
Therefore it is but little news
That put this hurry in my shoes."

And hurrying to the south he came
To that high hill the herdsmen name
The Hill Seat of Leighin, because
Some god or king had made the laws

That held the land together there,
In old times among the clouds of the air.

That old man climbed; the day grew dim;
Two swans came flying up to him
Linked by a gold chain each to each
And with low murmuring laughing speech
Alighted on the windy grass.
They knew him: his changed body was
Tall, proud and ruddy, and light wings
Were hovering over the harp strings
That Etain, Midhir's wife, had wove
In the hid place, being crazed by love.

What shall I call them? fish that swim
Scale rubbing scale where light is dim
By a broad water-lily leaf;
Or mice in the one wheaten sheaf
Forgotten at the threshing place;
Or birds lost in the one clear space
Of morning light in a dim sky;
Or it may be, the eyelids of one eye
Or the door pillars of one house,
Or two sweet blossoming apple boughs
That have one shadow on the ground;
Or the two strings that made one sound
Where that wise harper's finger ran;
For this young girl and this young man

Have happiness without an end
Because they have made so good a friend.

They know all wonders, for they pass
The towery gates of Gorias
And Findrias and Falias
And long-forgotten Murias,
Among the giant kings whose hoard
Cauldron and spear and stone and sword
Was robbed before Earth gave the wheat;
Wandering from broken street to street
They come where some huge watcher is
And tremble with their love and kiss.

They know undying things, for they
Wander where earth withers away,
Though nothing troubles the great streams
But light from the pale stars, and gleams
From the holy orchards, where there is none
But fruit that is of precious stone,
Or apples of the sun and moon.

What were our praise to them: they eat
Quiet's wild heart, like daily meat,
Who when night thickens are afloat
On dappled skins in a glass boat
Far out under a windless sky,
While over them birds of Aengus fly,

And over the tiller and the prow
And waving white wings to and fro
Awaken wanderings of light air
To stir their coverlet and their hair.

And poets found, old writers say,
A yew tree where his body lay,
But a wild apple hid the grass
With its sweet blossom where hers was;
And being in good heart, because
A better time had come again
After the deaths of many men,
And that long fighting at the ford,
They wrote on tablets of thin board,
Made of the apple and the yew,
All the love stories that they knew.

Let rush and bird cry out their fill
Of the harper's daughter if they will,
Beloved, I am not afraid of her
She is not wiser nor lovelier,
And you are more high of heart than she
For all her wanderings over-sea;
But I'd have bird and rush forget
Those other two, for never yet
Has lover lived but longed to wive
Like them that are no more alive.

THE HARP OF AENGUS

Edain came out of Midher's hill, and lay
Beside young Aengus in his tower of glass,
Where time is drowned in odour-laden winds
And druid moons, and murmuring of boughs,
And sleepy boughs, and boughs where apples made
Of opal and ruby and pale chrysolite
Awake unsleeping fires; and wove seven strings,
Sweet with all music, out of his long hair,
Because her hands had been made wild by love;
When Midher's wife had changed her to a fly,
He made a harp with druid apple wood
That she among her winds might know he wept;
And from that hour he has watched over none
But faithful lovers.

THE GREY ROCK

Poets with whom I learned my trade,
Companions of the Cheshire Cheese,
Here's an old story I've re-made,
Imagining 'twould better please
Your ears than stories now in fashion,
Though you may think I waste my breath
Pretending that there can be passion
That has more life in it than death,
And though at bottling of your wine
The bow-legged Goban had no say;
The moral's yours because it's mine.

When cups went round at close of day –
Is not that how good stories run? –
Somewhere within some hollow hill,
If books speak truth in Slievenamon,
But let that be, the gods were still
And sleepy, having had their meal,
And smoky torches made a glare
On painted pillars, on a deal
Of fiddles and of flutes hung there
By the ancient holy hands that brought them
From murmuring Murias, on cups –
Old Goban hammered them and wrought them,
And put his pattern round their tops
To hold the wine they buy of him.

But from the juice that made them wise
All those had lifted up the dim
Imaginations of their eyes,
For one that was like woman made
Before their sleepy eyelids ran
And trembling with her passion said,
"Come out and dig for a dead man,
Who's burrowing somewhere in the ground,
And mock him to his face and then
Hollo him on with horse and hound,
For he is the worst of all dead men."

We should be dazed and terror struck,
If we but saw in dreams that room,
Those wine-drenched eyes, and curse our luck
That emptied all our days to come.
I knew a woman none could please,
Because she dreamed when but a child
Of men and women made like these;
And after, when her blood ran wild,
Had ravelled her own story out,
And said, "In two or in three years
I need must marry some poor lout,"
And having said it burst in tears.
Since, tavern comrades, you have died,
Maybe your images have stood,
Mere bone and muscle thrown aside,
Before that roomful or as good.

You had to face your ends when young –
'Twas wine or women, or some curse –
But never made a poorer song
That you might have a heavier purse,
Nor gave loud service to a cause
That you might have a troop of friends.
You kept the Muses' sterner laws,
And unrelenting faced your ends,
And therefore earned the right – and yet
Dowson and Johnson most I praise –
To troop with those the world's forgot,
And copy their proud steady gaze.

"The Danish troop was driven out
Between the dawn and dusk," she said;
"Although the event was long in doubt,
Although the King of Ireland's dead
And half the kings, before sundown
All was accomplished."

            "When this day
Murrough, the King of Ireland's son,
Foot after foot was giving way,
He and his best troops back to back
Had perished there, but the Danes ran,
Stricken with panic from the attack,
The shouting of an unseen man;
And being thankful Murrough found,

Led by a footsole dipped in blood
That had made prints upon the ground,
Where by old thorn trees that man stood;
And though when he gazed here and there,
He had but gazed on thorn trees, spoke,
'Who is the friend that seems but air
And yet could give so fine a stroke?'
Thereon a young man met his eye,
Who said, 'Because she held me in
Her love, and would not have me die,
Rock-nurtured Aoife took a pin,
And pushing it into my shirt,
Promised that for a pin's sake,
No man should see to do me hurt;
But there it's gone; I will not take
The fortune that had been my shame
Seeing, King's son, what wounds you have.'
'Twas roundly spoke, but when night came
He had betrayed me to his grave,
For he and the King's son were dead.
I'd promised him two hundred years,
And when for all I'd done or said –
And these immortal eyes shed tears –
He claimed his country's need was most,
I'd save his life, yet for the sake
Of a new friend he has turned a ghost.
What does he care if my heart break?
I call for spade and horse and hound

That we may harry him." Thereon
She cast herself upon the ground
And rent her clothes and made her moan:
"Why are they faithless when their might
Is from the holy shades that rove
The grey rock and the windy light?
Why should the faithfullest heart most love
The bitter sweetness of false faces?
Why must the lasting love what passes,
Why are the gods by men betrayed!"

But thereon every god stood up
With a slow smile and without sound,
And stretching forth his arm and cup
To where she moaned upon the ground,
Suddenly drenched her to the skin;
And she with Goban's wine adrip,
No more remembering what had been,
Stared at the gods with laughing lip.

I have kept my faith, though faith was tried,
To that rock-born, rock-wandering foot,
And the world's altered since you died,
And I am in no good repute
With the loud host before the sea,
That think sword strokes were better meant
Than lover's music – let that be,
So that the wandering foot's content.

THE TWO KINGS

King Eochaid came at sundown to a wood
Westward of Tara. Hurrying to his queen
He had out-ridden his war-wasted men
That with empounded cattle trod the mire.
Where certain beeches mixed a pale green light
With the ground-ivy's blue, he saw a stag
Whiter than curds, its eyes the tint of the sea.
Because it stood upon his path and seemed
More hands in height than any stag in the world
He sat with tightened rein and loosened mouth
Upon his trembling horse, then drove the spur
But the stag stooped and ran at him, and passed,
Rending the horse's flank. King Eochaid reeled
Then drew his sword to hold its levelled point
Against the stag. When horn and steel were met
The horn resounded as though it had been silver,
A sweet, miraculous, terrifying sound.
Horn locked in sword, they tugged and
    struggled there
As though a stag and unicorn were met
In Africa on Mountain of the Moon,
Until at last the double horns, drawn backward,
Butted below the single and so pierced
The entrails of the horse. Dropping his sword
King Eochaid seized the horns in his strong hands
And stared into the sea-green eye, and so

Hither and thither to and fro they trod
Till all the place was beaten into mire.
The strong thigh and the agile thigh were met,
The hands that gathered up the might of the world,
And hoof and horn that had sucked in their speed
Amid the elaborate wilderness of the air.
Through bush they plunged and over ivied root,
And where the stone struck fire, while in the leaves
A squirrel whinnied and a bird screamed out;
But when at last he forced those sinewy flanks
Against a beech bole, he threw down the beast
And knelt above it with drawn knife. On the instant
It vanished like a shadow, and a cry
So mournful that it seemed the cry of one
Who had lost some unimaginable treasure
Wandered between the blue and the green leaf
And climbed into the air, crumbling away,
Till all had seemed a shadow or a vision
But for the trodden mire, the pool of blood,
The disembowelled horse.

            King Eochaid ran,
Toward peopled Tara, nor stood to draw his breath
Until he came before the painted wall,
The posts of polished yew, circled with bronze,
Of the great door; but though the hanging lamps
Showed their faint light through the
   unshuttered windows,

Nor door, nor mouth, nor slipper made a noise,
Nor on the ancient beaten paths, that wound
From well-side or from plough-land, was there noise;
And there had been no sound of living thing
Before him or behind, but that far-off
On the horizon edge bellowed the herds.
Knowing that silence brings no good to kings,
And mocks returning victory, he passed
Between the pillars with a beating heart
And saw where in the midst of the great hall
Pale-faced, alone upon a bench, Edain
Sat upright with a sword before her feet.
Her hands on either side had gripped the bench,
Her eyes were cold and steady, her lips tight.
Some passion had made her stone. Hearing a foot
She started and then knew whose foot it was;
But when he thought to take her in his arms
She motioned him afar, and rose and spoke:
"I have sent among the fields or to the woods
The fighting men and servants of this house,
For I would have your judgment upon one
Who is self-accused. If she be innocent
She would not look in any known man's face
Till judgment has been given, and if guilty,
Will never look again on known man's face."
And at these words he paled, as she had paled,
Knowing that he should find upon her lips
The meaning of that monstrous day.

Then she:
"You brought me where your brother Ardan sat
Always in his one seat, and bid me care him
Through that strange illness that had fixed him there,
And should he die to heap his burial mound
And carve his name in Ogham." Eochaid said,
"If he be living still the whole world's mine
But if not living, half the world is lost."
"I bid them make his bed under this roof
And carried him his food with my own hands,
And so the weeks passed by. But when I said
'What is this trouble?' he would answer nothing,
Though always at my words his trouble grew;
And I but asked the more, till he cried out,
Weary of many questions: 'There are things
That make the heart akin to the dumb stone.'
Then I replied: 'Although you hide a secret,
Hopeless and dear, or terrible to think on,
Speak it, that I may send through the wide world
For medicine.' Thereon he cried aloud:
'Day after day you question me, and I,
Because there is such a storm amid my thoughts
I shall be carried in the gust, command,
Forbid, beseech and waste my breath.' Then I,
'Although the thing that you have hid were evil,
The speaking of it could be no great wrong,
And evil must it be, if done 'twere worse
Than mound and stone that keep all virtue in,

And loosen on us dreams that waste our life,
Shadows and shows that can but turn the brain.'
But finding him still silent I stooped down
And whispering that none but he should hear,
Said: 'If a woman has put this on you,
My men, whether it please her or displease,
And though they have to cross the Loughlan waters
And take her in the middle of armed men,
Shall make her look upon her handiwork,
That she may quench the rick she has fired;
    and though
She may have worn silk clothes, or worn a crown,
She'll not be proud, knowing within her heart
That our sufficient portion of the world
Is that we give, although it be brief giving,
Happiness to children and to men.'
Then he, driven by his thought beyond his thought,
And speaking what he would not though he would,
Sighed: 'You, even you yourself, could work the cure!'
And at those words I rose and I went out
And for nine days he had food from other hands,
And for nine days my mind went whirling round
The one disastrous zodiac, muttering
That the immedicable mound's beyond
Our questioning, beyond our pity even.
But when nine days had gone I stood again
Before his chair and bending down my head
Told him, that when Orion rose, and all

The women of his household were asleep,
To go – for hope would give his limbs the power –
To an old empty woodman's house that's hidden
Close to a clump of beech trees in the wood
Westward of Tara, there to await a friend
That could, as he had told her, work his cure
And would be no harsh friend.

                When night had deepened,
I groped my way through boughs, and over roots,
Till oak and hazel ceased and beech began,
And found the house, a sputtering torch within,
And stretched out sleeping on a pile of skins
Ardan, and though I called to him and tried
To shake him out of sleep, I could not rouse him.
I waited till the night was on the turn,
Then fearing that some labourer, on his way
To plough or pasture-land, might see me there,
Went out.

              Among the ivy-covered rocks,
As on the blue light of a sword, a man
Who had unnatural majesty, and eyes
Like the eyes of some great kite scouring the woods,
Stood on my path. Trembling from hand to foot
I gazed at him like grouse upon a kite,
But with a voice that had unnatural music,
'A weary wooing and a long,' he said,
'Speaking of love through other lips and looking
Under the eyelids of another, for it was my craft

That put a passion in the sleeper there,
And when I had got my will and drawn you here,
Where I may speak to you alone, my craft
Sucked up the passion out of him again
And left mere sleep. He'll wake when the sun wakes,
Push out his vigorous limbs and rub his eyes,
And wonder what has ailed him these twelve months.'
I cowered back upon the wall in terror,
But that sweet-sounding voice ran on: 'Woman,
I was your husband when you rode the air,
Danced in the whirling foam and in the dust,
In days you have not kept in memory,
Being betrayed into a cradle, and I come
That I may claim you as my wife again.'
I was no longer terrified, his voice
Had half awakened some old memory,
Yet answered him: 'I am King Eochaid's wife
And with him have found every happiness
Women can find.' With a most masterful voice,
That made the body seem as it were a string
Under a bow, he cried: 'What happiness
Can lovers have that know their happiness
Must end at the dumb stone? But where we build
Our sudden palaces in the still air
Pleasure itself can bring no weariness,
Nor can time waste the cheek, nor is there foot
That has grown weary of the whirling dance,
Nor an unlaughing mouth, but mine that mourns,

Among those mouths that sing their
        sweethearts' praise,
Your empty bed.' 'How should I love,' I answered,
'Were it not that when the dawn has lit my bed
And shown my husband sleeping there, I have sighed,
"Your strength and nobleness will pass away."
Or how should love be worth its pains were it not
That when he has fallen asleep within my arms,
Being wearied out, I love in man the child?
What can they know of love that do not know
She builds her nest upon a narrow ledge
Above a windy precipice?' Then he:
'Seeing that when you come to the death-bed
You must return, whether you would or no,
This human life blotted from memory,
Why must I live some thirty, forty years,
Alone with all this useless happiness?'
Thereon he seized me in his arms, but I
Thrust him away with both my hands and cried,
'Never will I believe there is any change
Can blot out of my memory this life
Sweetened by death, but if I could believe
That were a double hunger in my lips
For what is doubly brief.'

                        And now the shape,
My hands were pressed to, vanished suddenly.
I staggered, but a beech tree stayed my fall,
And clinging to it I could hear the cocks
Crow upon Tara."

                        King Eochaid bowed his head
And thanked her for her kindness to his brother,
For that she promised, and for that refused.

Thereon the bellowing of the empounded herds
Rose round the walls, and through the bronze-
    ringed door
Jostled and shouted those war-wasted men,
And in the midst King Eochaid's brother stood.
He'd heard that din on the horizon's edge
And ridden towards it, being ignorant.

THE THREE BEGGARS

"Though to my feathers in the wet,
I have stood here from break of day,
I have not found a thing to eat
For only rubbish comes my way.
Am I to live on lebeen-lone?"
Muttered the old crane of Gort.
"For all my pains on lebeen-lone."

King Guari walked amid his court
The palace-yard and river-side
And there to three old beggars said:
"You that have wandered far and wide
Can ravel out what's in my head.
Do men who least desire get most,
Or get the most who most desire?"
A beggar said: "They get the most
Whom man or devil cannot tire,
And what could make their muscles taut
Unless desire had made them so."
But Guari laughed with secret thought,
"If that be true as it seems true,
One of you three is a rich man,
For he shall have a thousand pounds
Who is first asleep, if but he can
Sleep before the third noon sounds."
And thereon merry as a bird,

With his old thoughts King Guari went
From river-side and palace-yard
And left them to their argument.
"And if I win" one beggar said,
"Though I am old I shall persuade
A pretty girl to share my bed",
The second: "I shall learn a trade";
The third: "I'll hurry to the course
Among the other gentlemen,
And lay it all upon a horse";
"But now that I have thought again,
There is a solid dignity
About a farm," the second cried.

The exorbitant dreams of beggary,
That idleness had borne to pride,
Sang through their teeth from noon to noon;
And when the second twilight brought
The frenzy of the beggars' moon
They closed their blood-shot eyes for naught.
One beggar cried: "You're shamming sleep."
And thereupon their anger grew,
Till they were whirling in a heap.

They'd mauled and bitten the night through
Or sat upon their heels to rail,
And when old Guari came and stood
Before the three to end this tale,

They were commingling lice and blood.
"Time's up," he cried, and all the three
With blood-shot eyes upon him stared.
"Time's up," he cried, and all the three
Fell down upon the dust and snored.

"Maybe I shall be lucky yet,
Now they are silent," said the crane.
"Though to my feathers in the wet,
I've stood as I were made of stone
And seen the rubbish run about,
It's certain there are trout somewhere
And maybe I shall take a trout
If but I do not seem to care."

THE HOUR BEFORE DAWN

A one-legged, one-armed, one-eyed man
A bundle of rags upon a crutch
Stumbled on windy Cruachan
Cursing the wind. It was as much
As the one sturdy leg could do
To keep him upright while he cursed.
He counted, where long years ago
Queen Maeve's nine Maines had been nursed.
A pair of lapwings, one old sheep
And not a house to the plain's edge,
When close to his right hand a heap
Of grey stones and a rocky ledge
Reminded him that he could make,
If he but shifted a few stones,
A shelter till the daylight broke.
But while he fumbled with the stones
They toppled over; "Were it not
I have a lucky wooden shin
I had been hurt," the old beggar thought
And thereon saw, where stones had been
A dark deep hole in the rock's face,
Trembled and gasped and should have run
Being certain it was no right place
But the Hell Mouth at Cruachan
And stuffed with all that's old and bad;
And yet stood still, because inside

He had seen a red-haired jolly lad
In some outlandish coat beside
A ladle and a tub of beer,
Plainly no phantom by his look;
So with a laugh at his own fear
He crawled into that pleasant nook.
Young Red-head stretched himself to yawn
And murmured, "May God curse the night
That's grown uneasy near the dawn
So that it seems even I sleep light;
And who are you that wakens me?
Has one of Maeve's nine brawling sons
Grown tired of his own company?
But let him keep his grave for once
I have to find the sleep I have lost."
And then at last being wide awake,
"I took you for a brawling ghost,
Say what you please, but from day-break
I'll sleep another century."
The beggar deaf to all but hope
Went down upon a hand and knee
And took the wooden ladle up
And would have dipped it in the beer
But the other pushed his hand aside,
"Before you have dipped it in the beer
That sacred Goban brewed," he cried
"I'll have my say, till I am able
To judge if a light sleeping fool

Would have his fill out of my ladle
To make a clatter in the hole
In the bad hour before the dawn.
You've but to drink the beer and say
I'll sleep until the winter's gone,
Or maybe, to Midsummer Day
And so it will be. At the first
I waited so for that or this –
Because the weather was a-cursed
Or I had no woman there to kiss,
And slept for half a year or so;
But year by year I found that less
Gave me such pleasure I'd forego
Even a half hour's nothingness,
And when at one year's end I found
I had not waked a single minute
I chose this burrow under ground
And sleep away all Time within it.
My sleep were now nine centuries
But for those mornings when I find
The lapwing at their foolish cries
And the sheep bleating at the wind
As when I also played the fool."

The beggar in a rage began
Upon his hunkers in the hole
"It's plain that you are no right man
To mock at everything I love

As if it were not worth the doing.
I'd have a merry life enough
If a good Easter wind were blowing,
And though the winter wind is bad
I should not be too down in the mouth
For anything you did or said
If but this wind were in the south."
But the other cried, "You long for spring
Or that the wind would shift a point
And do not know that you would bring,
If time were suppler in the joint,
Neither the spring nor the south wind
But the hour when you shall pass away
And leave no smoking wick behind,
For all life longs for the Last Day
And there's no man but cocks his ear
To know when Michael's trumpet cries
That flesh and bone may disappear,
And souls as if they were but sighs,
And there be nothing but God left;
But I alone being blessed keep
Like some old rabbit to my cleft
And wait Him in a drunken sleep."
He dipped his ladle in the tub
And drank and yawned and stretched him out.

The other shouted, "You would rob
My life of every pleasant thought

And every comfortable thing
And so take that and that." Thereon
He gave him a great pummelling,
But might have pummelled at a stone
For all the sleeper knew or cared;
And after heaped the stones again
And cursed and prayed, and prayed and cursed
"Oh God if he got loose!" And then
In fury and in panic fled
From the Hell Mouth at Cruachan
And gave God thanks that overhead
The clouds were brightening with the dawn.

THE COLLAR-BONE OF A HARE

Would I could cast a sail on the water
Where many a king has gone
And many a king's daughter,
And alight at the comely trees and the lawn,
The playing upon pipes and the dancing,
And learn that the best thing is
To change my loves while dancing
And pay but a kiss for a kiss.

I would find by the edge of that water
The collar-bone of a hare
Worn thin by the lapping of water,
And pierce it through with a gimlet and stare
At the old bitter world where they marry in churches,
And laugh over the untroubled water
At all who marry in churches,
Through the white thin bone of a hare.

CUCHULAIN THE GIRL AND THE FOOL

THE GIRL

I am jealous of the looks men turn on you
For all men love your worth; and I must rage
At my own image in the looking-glass
That's so unlike myself that when you praise it
It is as though you praise another, or even
Mock me with praise of my mere opposite;
And when I wake towards morn I dread myself
For the heart cries that what deception wins
My cruelty must keep; and so begone
If you have seen that image and not my worth.

CUCHULAIN

All men have praised my strength but not my worth.

THE GIRL

If you are no more strength than I am beauty
I will find out some cavern in the hills
And live among the ancient holy men,
For they at least have all men's reverence
And have no need of cruelty to keep
What no deception won.

CUCHULAIN

                    I have heard them say
That men have reverence for their holiness
And not their worth.

THE GIRL
                         God loves us for our worth;
But what care I that long for a man's love.

THE FOOL BY THE ROADSIDE
When my days that have
From cradle run to grave
From grave to cradle run instead;
When thoughts that a fool
Has wound upon a spool
Are but loose thread, are but loose thread;

When cradle and spool are past
And I mere shade at last
Coagulate of stuff
Transparent like the wind,
I think that I may find
A faithful love, a faithful love.

LEDA AND THE SWAN

A rush, a sudden wheel, and hovering still
The bird descends and her frail thighs are pressed
By the webbed toes, and that all powerful bill
Has laid her helpless face upon his breast.
How can those terrified vague fingers push
The feathered glory from her loosening thighs!
All the stretched body's laid on the white rush
And feels the strange heart beating where it lies;
A shudder in the loins engenders there
The broken wall, the burning roof and tower
And Agamemnon dead.
                        Being so caught up,
So mastered by the brute blood of the air,
Did she put on his knowledge with his power
Before the indifferent beak could let her drop?

COUNTRY, CULTURE
& POLITICS
❊

THE BALLAD OF FATHER O'HART

Good Father John O'Hart
In penal days rode out
To a shoneen who had free lands
And his own snipe and trout.

In trust took he John's lands;
Sleiveens were all his race;
And he gave them as dowers to his daughters,
And they married beyond their place.

But Father John went up,
And Father John went down;
And he wore small holes in his shoes,
And he wore large holes in his gown.

All loved him, only the shoneen,
Whom the devils have by the hair,
From the wives, and the cats, and the children,
To the birds in the white of the air.

The birds, for he opened their cages
As he went up and down;
And he said with a smile, "Have peace now";
And he went his way with a frown.

But if when any one died
Came keeners hoarser than rooks,
He bade them give over their keening;
For he was a man of books.

And these were the works of John,
When weeping score by score,
People came into Coloony;
For he'd died at ninety-four.

There was no human keening;
The birds from Knocknarea
And the world round Knocknashee
Came keening in that day.

The young birds and old birds
Came flying, heavy and sad;
Keening in from Tiraragh,
Keening from Ballinafad;

Keening from Inishmurray,
Nor stayed for bite or sup;
This way were all reproved
Who dig old customs up.

THE ROSE OF BATTLE

Rose of all Roses, Rose of all the World!
The tall thought-woven sails, that flap unfurled
Above the tide of hours, trouble the air,
And God's bell buoyed to be the water's care;
While hushed from fear, or loud with hope, a band
With blown, spray-dabbled hair gather at hand.
Turn if you may from battles never done,
I call, as they go by me one by one,
Danger no refuge holds; and war no peace,
For him who hears love sing and never cease,
Beside her clean-swept hearth, her quiet shade:
But gather all for whom no love hath made
A woven silence, or but came to cast
A song into the air, and singing past
To smile on the pale dawn; and gather you
Who have sought more than is in rain or dew
Or in the sun and moon, or on the earth,
Or sighs amid the wandering, starry mirth,
Or comes in laughter from the sea's sad lips
And wage God's battles in the long gray ships.
The sad, the lonely, the insatiable,
To these Old Night shall all her mystery tell;
God's bell has claimed them by the little cry
Of their sad hearts, that may not live nor die.

Rose of all Roses, Rose of all the World!
You, too, have come where the dim tides are hurled
Upon the wharves of sorrow, and heard ring
The bell that calls us on; the sweet far thing.
Beauty grown sad with its eternity
Made you of us, and of the dim gray sea.
Our long ships loose thought-woven sails and wait,
For God has bid them share an equal fate;
And when at last defeated in His wars,
They have gone down under the same white stars,
We shall no longer hear the little cry
Of our sad hearts, that may not live nor die.

THE LAKE ISLE OF INNISFREE

I will arise and go now, and go to Innisfree,
And a small cabin build there, of clay and
    wattles made:
Nine bean rows will I have there, a hive for the
    honey bee,
And live alone in the bee-loud glade.

And I shall have some peace there, for peace comes
    dropping slow,
Dropping from the veils of the morning to where the
    cricket sings;
There midnight's all a glimmer, and noon a
    purple glow,
And evening full of the linnet's wings.

I will arise and go now, for always night and day
I hear lake water lapping with low sounds by
    the shore;
While I stand on the roadway, or on the pavements gray,
I hear it in the deep heart's core.

THE DEDICATION TO A BOOK OF STORIES SELECTED FROM THE IRISH NOVELISTS

There was a green branch hung with many a bell
When her own people ruled in wave-worn Eire;
And from its murmuring greenness, calm of faery,
A Druid kindness, on all hearers fell.

It charmed away the merchant from his guile,
And turned the farmer's memory from his cattle,
And hushed in sleep the roaring ranks of battle,
For all who heard it dreamed a little while.

Ah, Exiles wandering over many seas,
Spinning at all times Eire's good to-morrow!
Ah, worldwide Nation, always growing Sorrow!
I also bear a bell branch full of ease.

I tore it from green boughs winds tossed and hurled,
Green boughs of tossing always, weary, weary!
I tore it from the green boughs of old Eire,
The willow of the many-sorrowed world.

Ah, Exiles, wandering over many lands!
My bell branch murmurs: the gay bells bring laughter,
Leaping to shake a cobweb from the rafter;
The sad bells bow the forehead on the hands.

A honeyed ringing: under the new skies
They bring you memories of old village faces,
Cabins gone now, old well-sides, old dear places;
And men who loved the cause that never dies.

TO IRELAND IN THE COMING TIMES

Know, that I would accounted be
True brother of that company,
Who sang to sweeten Ireland's wrong,
Ballad and story, rann and song;
Nor be I any less of them,
Because the red-rose-bordered hem
Of her, whose history began
Before God made the angelic clan,
Trails all about the written page;
For in the world's first blossoming age
The light fall of her flying feet
Made Ireland's heart begin to beat;
And still the starry candles flare
To help her light foot here and there;
And still the thoughts of Ireland brood
Upon her holy quietude.

Nor may I less be counted one
With Davis, Mangan, Ferguson,
Because to him, who ponders well,
My rhymes more than their rhyming tell
Of the dim wisdoms old and deep,
That God gives unto man in sleep.
For the elemental beings go
About my table to and fro.
In flood and fire and clay and wind,

They huddle from man's pondering mind;
Yet he who treads in austere ways
May surely meet their ancient gaze.
Man ever journeys on with them
After the red-rose-bordered hem.
Ah, faeries, dancing under the moon,
A Druid land, a Druid tune!

While still I may, I write for you
The love I lived, the dream I knew.
From our birthday, until we die,
Is but the winking of an eye;
And we, our singing and our love,
The mariners of night above,
And all the wizard things that go
About my table to and fro.
Are passing on to where may be,
In truth's consuming ecstasy
No place for love and dream at all;
For God goes by with white foot-fall.
I cast my heart into my rhymes,
That you, in the dim coming times,
May know how my heart went with them
After the red-rose-bordered hem.

THE FIDDLER OF DOONEY

When I play on my fiddle in Dooney,
Folk dance like a wave of the sea;
My cousin is priest in Kilvarnet,
My brother in Moharabuiee.

I passed my brother and cousin:
They read in their books of prayer;
I read in my book of songs
I bought at the Sligo fair.

When we come at the end of time,
To Peter sitting in state,
He will smile on the three old spirits,
But call me first through the gate;
For the good are always the merry,
Save by an evil chance,
And the merry love the fiddle
And the merry love to dance:

And when the folk there spy me,
They will all come up to me,
With "Here is the fiddler of Dooney!"
And dance like a wave of the sea.

IN THE SEVEN WOODS

I have heard the pigeons of the Seven Woods
Make their faint thunder, and the garden bees
Hum in the lime tree flowers; and put away
The unavailing outcries and the old bitterness
That empty the heart. I have forgot awhile
Tara uprooted, and new commonness
Upon the throne and crying about the streets
And hanging its paper flowers from post to post,
Because it is alone of all things happy.
I am contented for I know that Quiet
Wanders laughing and eating her wild heart
Among pigeons and bees, while that Great Archer,
Who but awaits His hour to shoot, still hangs
A cloudy quiver over Parc-na-Lee.

THE SONG OF RED HANRAHAN

The old brown thorn trees break in two high over
    Cummen Strand
Under a bitter black wind that blows from the
    left hand,
Our courage breaks like an old tree in a black wind
    and dies;
But we have hidden in our hearts the flame out of
    the eyes
Of Cathleen the daughter of Houlihan.

The wind has bundled up the clouds high
    over Knocknarea
And thrown the thunder on the stones for all that
    Maeve can say.
Angers that are like noisy clouds have set our
    hearts abeat;
But we have all bent low and low and kissed the
    quiet feet
Of Cathleen the daughter of Houlihan.

The yellow pool has overflowed high up on Clooth-
    na-Bare,
For the wet winds are blowing out of the clinging air;
Like heavy flooded waters our bodies and our blood;
But purer than a tall candle before the Holy Rood
Is Cathleen the daughter of Houlihan.

TO LADY GREGORY

I walked among the seven woods of Coole,
Shan-walla, where a willow-bordered pond
Gathers the wild duck from the winter dawn;
Shady Kyle-dortha; sunnier Kyle-na-gno,
Where many hundred squirrels are as happy
As though they had been hidden by green boughs,
Where old age cannot find them; Pairc-na-lea,
Where hazel and ash and privet blind the paths;
Dim Pairc-na-carraig, where the wild bees fling
Their sudden fragrances on the green air;
Dim Pairc-na-tarav, where enchanted eyes
Have seen immortal, mild, proud shadows walk;
Dim Inchy wood, that hides badger and fox
And marten-cat, and borders that old wood
Wise Biddy Early called the wicked wood:
Seven odours, seven murmurs, seven woods.
I had not eyes like those enchanted eyes,
Yet dreamed that beings happier than men
Moved round me in the shadows, and at night
My dreams were cloven by voices and by fires;
And the images I have woven in this story
Of Forgael and Dectora and the empty waters
Moved round me in the voices and the fires,
And more I may not write of, for they that cleave
The waters of sleep can make a chattering tongue
Heavy like stone, their wisdom being half silence.

How shall I name you, immortal, mild,
    proud shadows?
I only know that all we know comes from you,
And that you come from Eden on flying feet.
Is Eden far away, or do you hide
From human thought, as hares and mice and coneys
That run before the reaping-hook and lie
In the last ridge of the barley? Do our woods
And winds and ponds cover more quiet woods,
More shining winds, more star-glimmering ponds?
Is Eden out of time and out of space?
And do you gather about us when pale light
Shining on water and fallen among leaves,
And winds blowing from flowers, and whirr of feathers
And the green quiet, have uplifted the heart?

I have made this poem for you, that men may read it
Before they read of Forgael and Dectora,
As men in the old times, before the harps began,
Poured out wine for the high invisible ones.

NO SECOND TROY

Why should I blame her that she filled my days
With misery, or that she would of late
Have taught to ignorant men most violent ways,
Or hurled the little streets upon the great,
Had they but courage equal to desire?
What could have made her peaceful with a mind
That nobleness made simple as a fire,
With beauty like a tightened bow, a kind
That is not natural in an age like this,
Being high and solitary and most stern?
Why, what could she have done being what she is?
Was there another Troy for her to burn?

UPON A THREATENED HOUSE

How should the world be luckier if this house.
Where passion and precision have been one
Time out of mind, became too ruinous
To breed the lidless eye that loves the sun?
And the sweet laughing eagle thoughts that grow
Where wings have memory of wings, and all
That comes of the best knit to the best? although
Mean roof-trees were the sturdier for its fall.
How should their luck run high enough to reach
The gifts that govern men, and after these
To gradual Time's last gift, a written speech
Wrought of high laughter, loveliness and ease?

THESE ARE THE CLOUDS

These are the clouds about the fallen sun,
The majesty that shuts his burning eye;
The weak lay hand on what the strong has done,
Till that be tumbled that was lifted high
And discord follow upon unison,
And all things at one common level lie.
And therefore, friend, if your great race were run
And these things came, so much the more thereby
Have you made greatness your companion,
Although it be for children that you sigh:
These are the clouds about the fallen sun,
The majesty that shuts his burning eye.

AT GALWAY RACES

Out yonder, where the Race Course is,
Delight makes all of the one mind,
The riders upon the swift horses,
The field that closes in behind:
We too, had good attendance once,
Hearers and hearteners of the work;
Aye, horsemen for companions,
Before the merchant and the clerk
Breathed on the world with timid breath.
Sing on: sometime, and at some new moon
We'll learn that sleeping is not death,
Hearing the whole earth change its tune.
Its flesh being wild, and it again
Crying aloud as the race course is,
And we find hearteners among men
That ride upon horses.

TO A WEALTHY MAN, WHO PROMISED A SECOND SUBSCRIPTION IF IT WERE PROVED THE PEOPLE WANTED PICTURES

You gave but will not give again
Until enough of Paudeen's pence
By Biddy's halfpennies have lain
To be "some sort of evidence"
Before you'll put your guineas down
That things it were a pride to give
Are what the blind and ignorant town
Imagines best to make it thrive.
What cared Duke Ercole that bid
His mummers to the market place;
What th' onion-sellers thought or did
So that his Plautus set the pace
For the Italian comedies?
And Guidobaldo when he made
That grammar school of courtesies,
Where wit and beauty learned their trade
Upon Urbino's windy hill,
Had sent no runners to and fro
That he might learn the shepherds' will;
And when they drove out Cosimo,
Indifferent how the rancour ran.
He gave the hours they had set free
To Michelozzo's latest plan

For the San Marco Library;
Whence turbulent Italy should draw
Delight in Art whose end is peace
In logic and in natural law
By sucking at the dugs of Greece.

Your open hand but shows our loss,
For he knew better how to live.
Let Paudeens play at pitch and toss.
Look up in the sun's eye and give
What the exultant heart calls good
That some new day may breed the best
Because you gave, not what they would
But the right twigs for an eagle's nest!

SEPTEMBER, 1913

What need you, being come to sense.
But fumble in a greasy till
And add the halfpence to the pence
And prayer to shivering prayer, until
You have dried the marrow from the bone;
For men were born to pray and save,
Romantic Ireland's dead and gone,
It's with O'Leary in the grave.

Yet they were of a different kind
The names that stilled your childish play
They have gone about the world like win
But little time had they to pray
For whom the hangman's rope was spun,
And what, God help us, could they save:
Romantic Ireland's dead and gone,
It's with O'Leary in the grave.

Was it for this the wild geese spread
The grey wing upon every tide;
For this that all that blood was shed,
For this Edward Fitzgerald died,
And Robert Emmet and Wolfe Tone,
All that delirium of the brave;
Romantic Ireland's dead and gone,
It's with O'Leary in the grave.

Yet could we turn the years again,
And call those exiles as they were,
In all their loneliness and pain
You'd cry "some woman's yellow hair
Has maddened every mother's son":
They weighed so lightly what they gave,
But let them be, they're dead and gone,
They're with O'Leary in the grave.

TO A FRIEND WHOSE WORK HAS COME TO NOTHING

Now all the truth is out,
Be secret and take defeat
From any brazen throat,
For how can you compete,
Being honour bred, with one
Who were it proved he lies
Were neither shamed in his own
Nor in his neighbours' eyes;
Bred to a harder thing
Than Triumph, turn away
And like a laughing string
Whereon mad fingers play
Amid a place of stone,
Be secret and exult,
Because of all things known
That is most difficult.

PAUDEEN

Indignant at the fumbling wits, the obscure spite
Of our old Paudeen in his shop, I stumbled blind
Among the stones and thorn trees, under
    morning light,
Until a curlew cried and in the luminous wind
A curlew answered, and I was startled by the thought
That on the lonely height where all are in God's eye,
There cannot be, confusion of our sound forgot,
A single soul that lacks a sweet crystaline cry.

TO A SHADE

If you have revisited the town, thin Shade,
Whether to look upon your monument
(I wonder if the builder has been paid)
Or happier thoughted when the day is spent
To drink of that salt breath out of the sea
When grey gulls fly about instead of men,
And the gaunt houses put on majesty:
Let these content you and be gone again;
For they are at their old tricks yet.
                              A man
Of your own passionate serving kind who had brought
In his full hands what, had they only known,
Had given their children's children loftier thought
Sweeter emotion, working in their veins
Like gentle blood, has been driven from the place,
And insult heaped upon him for his pains
And for his open-handedness, disgrace;
An old foul mouth that once cried out on you
Herding the pack.
                              Unquiet wanderer
Draw the Glasnevin coverlet anew
About your head till the dust stops your ear,
The time for you to taste of that salt breath
And listen at the corners has not come;
You had enough of sorrow before death –
Away, away! You are safer in the tomb.

THE ATTACK ON 'THE PLAYBOY
OF THE WESTERN WORLD', 1907

Once, when midnight smote the air,
Eunuchs ran through Hell and met
Round about Hell's Gate to stare
At great Juan riding by;
And like these to rail and sweat
Staring on his sinewy thigh.

AN APPOINTMENT

Being out of heart with government
I took a broken root to fling
Where the proud, wayward squirrel went,
Taking delight that he could spring;
And he, with that low whinnying sound
That is like laughter, sprang again
And so to the other tree at a bound.
Nor the tame will, nor timid brain,
Bred that fierce tooth and cleanly limb
And threw him up to laugh on the bough;
No government appointed him.

THE PEOPLE

"What have I earned for all that work," I said,
"For all that I have done at my own charge?
The daily spite of this unmannerly town,
Where who has served the most is most defamed,
The reputation of his lifetime lost
Between the night and morning. I might have lived,
And you know well how great the longing has been.
Where every day my footfall should have lit
In the green shadow of Ferrara wall;
Or climbed among the images of the past –
The unperturbed and courtly images –
Evening and morning, the steep street of Urbino
To where the duchess and her people talked
The stately midnight through until they stood
In their great window looking at the dawn;
I might have had no friend that could not mix
Courtesy and passion into one like those
That saw the wicks grow yellow in the dawn;
I might have used the one substantial right
My trade allows: chosen my company,
And chosen what scenery had pleased me best."

Thereon my phoenix answered in reproof,
"The drunkards, pilferers of public funds.
All the dishonest crowd I had driven away,
When my luck changed and they dared meet my face,

Crawled from obscurity, and set upon me
Those I had served and some that I had fed;
Yet never have I, now nor any time,
Complained of the people."

        All I could reply
Was: "You, that have not lived in thought but deed,
Can have the purity of a natural force,
But I, whose virtues are the definitions
Of the analytic mind, can neither close
The eye of the mind nor keep my tongue
    from speech."

And yet, because my heart leaped at her words,
I was abashed, and now they come to mind
After nine years, I sink my head abashed.

TO A SQUIRREL AT KYLE-NA-GNO

Come play with me;
Why should you run
Through the shaking tree
As though I'd a gun
To strike you dead,
When all I would do
Is to scratch your head
And let you go.

ON BEING ASKED FOR A WAR POEM

I think it better that in times like these
A poet keep his mouth shut, for in truth
We have no gift to set a statesman right;
He has had enough of meddling who can please
A young girl in the indolence of her youth,
Or an old man upon a winter's night.

THE SCHOLARS

Bald heads forgetful of their sins,
Old, learned, respectable bald heads
Edit and annotate the lines
That young men, tossing on their beds,
Rhymed out in love's despair
To flatter beauty's ignorant ear.

They'll cough in the ink to the world's end;
Wear out the carpet with their shoes
Earning respect; have no strange friend;
If they have sinned nobody knows.
Lord, what would they say
Should their Catullus walk that way?

MICHAEL ROBARTES AND THE DANCER

HE
Opinion is not worth a rush;
In this altar-piece the knight,
Who grips his long spear so to push
That dragon through the fading light,
Loved the lady; and it's plain
The half-dead dragon was her thought,
That every morning rose again
And dug its claws and shrieked and fought.
Could the impossible come to pass
She would have time to turn her eyes,
Her lover thought, upon the glass
And on the instant would grow wise.

SHE
You mean they argued.

HE
          Put it so;
But bear in mind your lover's wage
Is what your looking-glass can show,
And that he will turn green with rage
At all that is not pictured there.

SHE
May I not put myself to college?

HE
Go pluck Athena by the hair;
For what mere book can grant a knowledge
With an impassioned gravity
Appropriate to that beating breast,
That vigorous thigh, that dreaming eye?
And may the devil take the rest.

SHE
And must no beautiful woman be
Learned like a man?

HE
                    Paul Veronese
And all his sacred company
Imagined bodies all their days
By the lagoon you love so much,
For proud, soft, ceremonious proof
That all must come to sight and touch;
While Michael Angelo's Sistine roof
His 'Morning' and his 'Night' disclose
How sinew that has been pulled tight,
Or it may be loosened in repose,
Can rule by supernatural right
Yet be but sinew.

SHE
                    I have heard said
There is great danger in the body.

HE
Did God in portioning wine and bread
Give man His thought or His mere body?

SHE
My wretched dragon is perplexed.

HE
I have principles to prove me right.
It follows from this Latin text
That blest souls are not composite,
And that all beautiful women may
Live in uncomposite blessedness,
And lead us to the like – if they
Will banish every thought, unless
The lineaments that please their view
When the long looking-glass is full,
Even from the foot-sole think it too.

SHE
They say such different things at school.

EASTER, 1916

I have met them at close of day
Coming with vivid faces
From counter or desk among grey
Eighteenth-century houses.
I have passed with a nod of the head
Or polite meaningless words,
Or have lingered awhile and said
Polite meaningless words,
And thought before I had done
Of a mocking tale or a gibe
To please a companion
Around the fire at the club,
Being certain that they and I
But lived where motley is worn:
All changed, changed utterly:
A terrible beauty is born.

That woman's days were spent
In ignorant good will,
Her nights in argument
Until her voice grew shrill.
What voice more sweet than hers
When young and beautiful,
She rode to harriers?
This man had kept a school
And rode our winged horse.

This other his helper and friend
Was coming into his force;
He might have won fame in the end,
So sensitive his nature seemed,
So daring and sweet his thought.
This other man I had dreamed
A drunken, vain-glorious lout.
He had done most bitter wrong
To some who are near my heart,
Yet I number him in the song;
He, too, has resigned his part
In the casual comedy;
He, too, has been changed in his turn,
Transformed utterly:
A terrible beauty is born.

Hearts with one purpose alone
Through summer and winter seem
Enchanted to a stone
To trouble the living stream.
The horse that comes from the road,
The rider, the birds that range
From cloud to tumbling cloud,
Minute by minute change;
A shadow of cloud on the stream
Changes minute by minute;
A horse-hoof slides on the brim,
And a horse plashes within it

Where long-legged moor-hens dive,
And hens to moor-cocks call.
Minute by minute they live:
The stone's in the midst of all.

Too long a sacrifice
Can make a stone of the heart.
O when may it suffice?
That is heaven's part, our part
To murmur name upon name,
As a mother names her child
When sleep at last has come
On limbs that had run wild.
What is it but nightfall?
No, no, not night but death;
Was it needless death after all?
For England may keep faith
For all that is done and said.
We know their dream; enough
To know they dreamed and are dead.
And what if excess of love
Bewildered them till they died?
I write it out in a verse –
MacDonagh and MacBride
And Connolly and Pearse
Now and in time to be,
Wherever green is worn,
Are changed, changed utterly:
A terrible beauty is born.

SIXTEEN DEAD MEN

O but we talked at large before
The sixteen men were shot,
But who can talk of give and take,
What should be and what not?
While those dead men are loitering there
To stir the boiling pot.

You say that we should still the land
Till Germany's overcome;
But who is there to argue that
Now Pearse is deaf and dumb?
And is their logic to outweigh
MacDonagh's bony thumb?

How could you dream they'd listen
That have an ear alone
For those new comrades they have found
Lord Edward and Wolfe Tone,
Or meddle with our give and take
That converse bone to bone.

THE ROSE TREE

"O words are lightly spoken"
Said Pearse to Connolly,
"Maybe a breath of politic words
Has withered our Rose Tree;
Or maybe but a wind that blows
Across the bitter sea."

"It needs to be but watered,"
James Connolly replied,
"To make the green come out again
And spread on every side,
And shake the blossom from the bud
To be the garden's pride."

"But where can we draw water"
Said Pearse to Connolly,
"When all the wells are parched away?
O plain as plain can be
There's nothing but our own red blood
Can make a right Rose Tree."

ON A POLITICAL PRISONER

She that but little patience knew,
From childhood on, had now so much
A grey gull lost its fear and flew
Down to her cell and there alit,
And there endured her fingers touch
And from her fingers ate its bit.

Did she in touching that lone wing
Recall the years before her mind
Became a bitter, an abstract thing,
Her thought some popular enmity:
Blind and leader of the blind
Drinking the foul ditch where they lie?

When long ago I saw her ride
Under Ben Bulban to the meet,
The beauty of her country-side
With all youth's lonely wildness stirred,
She seemed to have grown clean and sweet
Like any rock-bred, sea-borne bird:

Sea-borne, or balanced on the air
When first it sprang out of the nest
Upon some lofty rock to stare
Upon the cloudy canopy,
While under its storm-beaten breast
Cried out the hollows of the sea.

THE LEADERS OF THE CROWD

They must to keep their certainty accuse
All that are different of a base intent;
Pull down established honour; hawk for news
Whatever their loose phantasy invent
And murmur it with bated breath, as though
The abounding gutter had been Helicon
Or calumny a song. How can they know
Truth flourishes where the student's lamp has shone,
And there alone, that have no solitude?
So the crowd come they care not what may come.
They have loud music, hope every day renewed
And heartier loves; that lamp is from the tomb.

TOWARDS BREAK OF DAY

Was it the double of my dream
The woman that by me lay
Dreamed, or did we halve a dream
Under the first cold gleam of day?

I thought "there is a waterfall
Upon Ben Bulban side,
That all my childhood counted dear;
Were I to travel far and wide
I could not find a thing so dear."
My memories had magnified
So many times childish delight.

I would have touched it like a child
But knew my finger could but have touched
Cold stone and water. I grew wild
Even accusing heaven because
It had set down among its laws:
Nothing that we love over-much
Is ponderable to our touch.

I dreamed towards break of day,
The cold blown spray in my nostril.
But she that beside me lay
Had watched in bitterer sleep
The marvellous stag of Arthur,
That lofty white stag, leap
From mountain steep to steep.

THE SECOND COMING

Turning and turning in the widening gyre
The falcon cannot hear the falconer;
Things fall apart; the centre cannot hold;
Mere anarchy is loosed upon the world,
The blood-dimmed tide is loosed, and everywhere
The ceremony of innocence is drowned;
The best lack all conviction, while the worst
Are full of passionate intensity.

Surely some revelation is at hand;
Surely the Second Coming is at hand.
The Second Coming! Hardly are those words out
When a vast image out of Spiritus Mundi
Troubles my sight: a waste of desert sand;
A shape with lion body and the head of a man,
A gaze blank and pitiless as the sun,
Is moving its slow thighs, while all about it
Wind shadows of the indignant desert birds.

The darkness drops again but now I know
That twenty centuries of stony sleep
Were vexed to nightmare by a rocking cradle,
And what rough beast, its hour come round at last,
Slouches towards Bethlehem to be born?

A PRAYER FOR MY DAUGHTER

Once more the storm is howling and half hid
Under this cradle-hood and coverlid
My child sleeps on. There is no obstacle
But Gregory's Wood and one bare hill
Whereby the haystack and roof-levelling wind,
Bred on the Atlantic, can be stayed;
And for an hour I have walked and prayed
Because of the great gloom that is in my mind.

I have walked and prayed for this young child an hour
And heard the sea-wind scream upon the tower,
And under the arches of the bridge, and scream
In the elms above the flooded stream;
Imagining in excited reverie
That the future years had come,
Dancing to a frenzied drum,
Out of the murderous innocence of the sea.

May she be granted beauty and yet not
Beauty to make a stranger's eye distraught,
Or hers before a looking-glass, for such,
Being made beautiful overmuch,
Consider beauty a sufficient end,
Lose natural kindness and maybe
The heart-revealing intimacy
That chooses right and never find a friend.

Helen being chosen found life flat and dull
And later had much trouble from a fool,
While that great Queen, that rose out of the spray,
Being fatherless could have her way
Yet chose a bandy-legged smith for man.
It's certain that fine women eat
A crazy salad with their meat
Whereby the Horn of Plenty is undone.

In courtesy I'd have her chiefly learned;
Hearts are not had as a gift but hearts are earned
By those that are not entirely beautiful;
Yet many, that have played the fool
For beauty's very self, has charm made wise,
And many a poor man that has roved,
Loved and thought himself beloved,
From a glad kindness cannot take his eyes.

May she become a flourishing hidden tree
That all her thoughts may like the linnet be,
And have no business but dispensing round
Their magnanimities of sound,
Nor but in merriment begin a chase,
Nor but in merriment a quarrel.
Oh, may she live like some green laurel
Rooted in one dear perpetual place.

My mind, because the minds that I have loved,
The sort of beauty that I have approved,
Prosper but little, has dried up of late,
Yet knows that to be choked with hate
May well be of all evil chances chief.
If there's no hatred in a mind
Assault and battery of the wind
Can never tear the linnet from the leaf.

An intellectual hatred is the worst,
So let her think opinions are accursed.
Have I not seen the loveliest woman born
Out of the mouth of Plenty's horn,
Because of her opinionated mind
Barter that horn and every good
By quiet natures understood
For an old bellows full of angry wind?

Considering that, all hatred driven hence,
The soul recovers radical innocence
And learns at last that it is self-delighting,
Self-appeasing, self-affrighting,
And that its own sweet will is heaven's will;
She can, though every face should scowl
And every windy quarter howl
Or every bellows burst, be happy still.

And may her bride-groom bring her to a house
Where all's accustomed, ceremonious;
For arrogance and hatred are the wares
Peddled in the thoroughfares.
How but in custom and in ceremony
Are innocence and beauty born?
Ceremony's a name for the rich horn,
And custom for the spreading laurel tree.

A MEDITATION IN TIME OF WAR

For one throb of the Artery,
While on that old grey stone I sat
Under the old wind-broken tree,
I knew that One is animate
Mankind inanimate phantasy.

TO BE CARVED ON A STONE
AT BALLYLEE

I, the poet William Yeats,
With old mill boards and sea-green slates,
And smithy work from the Gort forge,
Restored this tower for my wife George;
And may these characters remain
When all is ruin once again.

THOUGHTS UPON THE PRESENT STATE OF THE WORLD

I

Many ingenious lovely things are gone
That seemed sheer miracle to the multitude;
Above the murderous treachery of the moon
Or all that wayward ebb and flow. There stood
Amid the ornamental bronze and stone
An ancient image made of olive wood;
And gone are Phidias' carven ivories
And all his golden grasshoppers and bees.

We too had many pretty toys when young;
A law indifferent to blame or praise
To bribe or threat; habits that made old wrong
Melt down, as it were wax in the sun's rays;
Public opinion ripening for so long
We thought it would outlive all future days.
O what fine thought we had because we thought
That the worst rogues and rascals had died out.

All teeth were drawn, all ancient tricks unlearned,
And a great army but a showy thing;
What matter that no cannon had been turned
Into a ploughshare; parliament and king
Thought that unless a little powder burned

The trumpeters might burst with trumpeting
And yet it lack all glory; and perchance
The guardsmen's drowsy chargers would not prance.

Now days are dragon-ridden, the nightmare
Rides upon sleep: a drunken soldiery
Can leave the mother, murdered at her door,
To crawl in her own blood, and go scot-free;
The night can sweat with terror as before
We pieced our thoughts into philosophy,
And planned to bring the world under a rule
Who are but weasels fighting in a hole.

He who can read the signs nor sink unmanned
Into the half-deceit of some intoxicant
From shallow wits, who knows no work can stand,
Whether health, wealth or peace of mind were spent
On master work of intellect or hand,
No honour leave its mighty monument,
Has but one comfort left: all triumph would
But break upon his ghostly solitude.

And other comfort were a bitter wound:
To be in love and love what vanishes.
Greeks were but lovers; all that country round
None dared admit, if such a thought were his,
Incendiary or bigot could be found
To burn that stump on the Acropolis,

Or break in bits the famous ivories
Or traffic in the grasshoppers or bees?

II

When Loie Fuller's Chinese dancers enwound
A shining web, a floating ribbon of cloth,
It seemed that a dragon of air
Had fallen among dancers, had whirled them round
Or hurried them off on its own furious path;
So the platonic year
Whirls out new right and wrong
Whirls in the old instead;
All men are dancers and their tread
Goes to the barbarous clangour of gong.

III

Some moralist or mythological poet
Compares the solitary soul to a swan;
I am content with that,
Contented that a troubled mirror show it
Before that brief gleam of its life be gone,
An image of its state;
The wings half spread for flight,
The breast thrust out in pride
Whether to play or to ride
Those winds that clamour of approaching night.

A man in his own secret meditation
Is lost amid the labyrinth that he has made
In art or politics;
Some platonist affirms that in the station
Where we should cast off body and trade
The ancient habit sticks,
And that if our works could
But vanish with our breath
That were a lucky death,
For triumph can but mar our solitude.

The swan has leaped into the desolate heaven:
That image can bring wildness, bring a rage
To end all things, to end
What my laborious life imagined, even
The half imagined, the half written page;
O but we dreamed to mend
Whatever mischief seemed
To afflict mankind, but now
That winds of winter blow
Learn that we were crack-pated when we dreamed.

IV

We, who seven years ago
Talked of honour and of truth,
Shriek with pleasure if we show
The weasel's twist, the weasel's tooth.

V

Come let us mock at the great
That had such burdens on the mind
And toiled so hard and late
To leave some monument behind,
Nor thought of the levelling wind.

Come let us mock at the wise;
With all those calendars whereon
They fixed old aching eyes,
They never saw how seasons run,
And now but gape at the sun.

Come let us mock at the good
That fancied goodness might be gay,
Grown tired of their solitude,
Upon some brand-new happy day:
Wind shrieked – and where are they?

Mock mockers after that
That would not lift a hand maybe
To help good, wise or great
To bar that foul storm out, for we
Traffic in mockery.

VI

Violence upon the roads: violence of horses;
Some few have handsome riders, are garlanded
On delicate sensitive ear or tossing mane,
But wearied running round and round in their courses
All break and vanish, and evil gathers head:
Herodias' daughters have returned again
A sudden blast of dusty wind and after
Thunder of feet, tumult of images,
Their purpose in the labyrinth of the wind;

And should some crazy hand dare touch a daughter
All turn with amorous cries, or angry cries,
According to the wind, for all are blind.
But now wind drops, dust settles; thereupon
There lurches past, his great eyes without thought
Under the shadow of stupid straw-pale locks,
That insolent fiend Robert Artisson
To whom the love-lorn Lady Kyteler brought
Bronzed peacock feathers, red combs of her cocks.

THE NEW FACES

If you, that have grown old were the first dead
Neither Caltapa tree nor scented lime
Should hear my living feet, nor would I tread
Where we wrought that shall break the teeth of time.
Let the new faces play what tricks they will
In the old rooms; night can outbalance day,
Our shadows rove the garden gravel still,
The living seem more shadowy than they.

A PRAYER FOR MY SON

Bid a strong ghost stand at the head
That my Michael may sleep sound,
Nor cry, nor turn in the bed
Till his morning meal come round;
And may departing twilight keep
All dread afar till morning's back
That his mother may not lack
Her fill of sleep.

Bid the ghost have sword in hand:
There are malicious things, although
Few dream that they exist,
Who have planned his murder, for they know
Of some most haughty deed or thought
That waits upon his future days,
And would through hatred of the bays
Bring that to nought.

Though You can fashion everything
From nothing every day, and teach
The morning stars to sing,
You have lacked articulate speech
To tell Your simplest want, and known,
Wailing upon a woman's knee,
All of that worst ignominy
Of flesh and bone;

And when through all the town there ran
The servants of Your enemy
A woman and a man,
Unless the Holy Writings lie,
Have borne You through the smooth and rough
And through the fertile and waste,
Protecting till the danger past
With human love.

MEDITATIONS IN TIME OF CIVIL WAR

I — *Ancestral Houses*

Surely among a rich man's flowering lawns,
Amid the rustle of his planted hills,
Life overflows without ambitious pains;
And rains down life until the basin spills,
And mounts more dizzy high the more it rains
As though to choose whatever shape it wills
And never stoop to a mechanical,
Or servile shape, at others' beck and call.

Mere dreams, mere dreams! Yet Homer had not Sung
Had he not found it certain beyond dreams
That out of life's own self-delight had sprung
The abounding glittering jet; though now it seems
As if some marvellous empty sea-shell flung
Out of the obscure dark of the rich streams,
And not a fountain, were the symbol which
Shadows the inherited glory of the rich.

Some violent bitter man, some powerful man
Called architect and artist in, that they,
Bitter and violent men, might rear in stone
The sweetness that all longed for night and day,
The gentleness none there had ever known;
But when the master's buried mice can play.

And maybe the great-grandson of that house
For all its bronze and marble's but a mouse.

O what if gardens where the peacock strays
With delicate feet upon old terraces,
Or else all Juno from an urn displays
Before the indifferent garden deities;
O what if levelled lawns and gravelled ways
Where slippered Contemplation finds his ease
And Childhood a delight for every sense,
But take our greatness with our violence?

What if the glory of escutcheoned doors,
And buildings that a haughtier age designed,
The pacing to and fro on polished floors
Amid great chambers and long galleries, lined
With famous portraits of our ancestors;
What if those things the greatest of mankind,
Consider most to magnify, or to bless,
But take our greatness with our bitterness?

II — My House

An ancient bridge, and a more ancient tower,
A farmhouse that is sheltered by its wall,
An acre of stony ground,
Where the symbolic rose can break in flower,
Old ragged elms, old thorns innumerable,

The sound of the rain or sound
Of every wind that blows,
The stilted water-hen
That plunged in stream again
Scared by the splashing of a dozen cows.

A winding stair, a chamber arched with stone,
A grey stone fireplace with an open hearth,
A candle and written page.
Il Penseroso's Platonist toiled on
In some like chamber, shadowing forth
How the daemonic rage
Imagined everything.
Benighted travellers
From markets and from fairs
Have seen his midnight candle glimmering.

The river rises, and it sinks again;
One hears the rumble of it far below
Under its rocky hole.
What Median, Persian, Babylonian,
In reverie, or in vision, saw
Symbols of the soul
Mind from mind has caught:
The subterranean streams,
Tower where a candle gleams,
A suffering passion and a labouring thought?

Two men have founded here. A man-at-arms
Gathered a score of horse and spent his days
In this tumultuous spot,
Where through long wars and sudden night alarms
His dwindling score and he seemed cast-a-ways
Forgetting and forgot;
And I, that after me
My bodily heirs may find,
To exalt a lonely mind,
Befitting emblems of adversity.

III — My Table

Two heavy trestles, and a board
Where Sato's gift, a changeless sword,
By pen and paper lies,
That it may moralise
My days out of their aimlessness.
A bit of an embroidered dress
Covers its wooden sheath.
Chaucer had not drawn breath
When it was forged. In Sato's house,
Curved like new moon, moon luminous
It lay five hundred years;
Yet if no change appears
No moon: only an aching heart
Conceives a changeless work of art.
Our learned men have urged

That when and where 'twas forged
A marvellous accomplishment,
In painting or in pottery, went
From father unto son
And through the centuries ran
And seemed unchanging like the sword.
Soul's beauty being most adored,
Men and their business took
Me soul's unchanging look;
For the most rich inheritor,
Knowing that none could pass heaven's door,
That loved inferior art,
Had such an aching heart
That he, although a country's talk
For silken clothes and stately walk,
Had waking wits; it seemed
Juno's peacock screamed.

IV — My Descendants

Having inherited a vigorous mind
From my old fathers, I must nourish dreams
And leave a woman and a man behind
As vigorous of mind, and yet it seems
Life scarce can cast a fragrance on the wind,
Scarce spread a glory to the morning beams,
But the torn petals strew the garden plot;
And there's but common greenness after that.

And what if my descendants lose the flower
Through natural declension of the soul,
Through too much business with the passing hour,
Through too much play, or marriage with a fool?
May this laborious stair and this stark tower
Become a roofless ruin that the owl
May build in the cracked masonry and cry
Her desolation to the desolate sky.

The Primum Mobile that fashioned us
Has made the very owls in circles move;
And I, that count myself most prosperous
Seeing that love and friendship are enough,
For an old neighbour's friendship chose the house
And decked and altered it for a girl's love,
And know whatever flourish and decline
These stones remain their monument and mine.

V — The Road at My Door

An affable Irregular,
A heavily-built Falstaffian man,
Comes cracking jokes of civil war
As though to die by gunshot were
The finest play under the sun.

A brown Lieutenant and his men,
Half dressed in national uniform,

Stand at my door, and I complain
Of the foul weather, hail and rain,
A pear-tree broken by the storm.

I count those feathered balls of soot
The moor-hen guides upon the stream,
To silence the envy in my thought;
And turn towards my chamber, caught
In the cold snows of a dream.

VI — *The Stare's Nest by My Window*

The bees build in the crevices
Of loosening masonry, and there
The mother birds bring grubs and flies.
My wall is loosening, honey bees,
Come build in the empty house of the stare.

We are closed in, and the key is turned
On our uncertainty; somewhere
A man is killed, or a house burned,
Yet no clear fact to be discerned:
Come build in the empty house of the stare.

A barricade of stone or of wood;
Some fourteen days of civil war;
Last night they trundled down the road
That dead young soldier in his blood:
Come build in the empty house of the stare.

We had fed the heart on fantasies,
The heart's grown brutal from the fare,
More substance in our enmities
Than in our love; oh, honey-bees,
Come build in the empty house of the stare.

VII — I See Phantoms of Hatred and of the Heart's Fullness and of the Coming Emptiness

I climb to the tower top and lean upon broken stone,
A mist that is like blown snow is sweeping over all,
Valley, river, and elms, under the light of a moon
That seems unlike itself, that seems unchangeable,
A glittering sword out of the east. A puff of wind
And those white glimmering fragments of the mist
    sweep by.
Frenzies, bewilder, reveries perturb the mind;
Monstrous familiar images swim to the mind's eye.

"Vengeance upon the murderers," the cry goes up
"Vengeance for Jacques Molay." In cloud-pale rags, or
    in lace,
The rage driven, rage tormented, and rage hungry troop
Trooper belabouring trooper, biting at arm or at face,
Plunges towards nothing, arms and fingers
    spreading wide
For the embrace of nothing; and I, my wits astray

Because of all that senseless tumult, all but cried
For vengeance on the murderers of Jacques Molay.

Their legs long, delicate and slender, aquamarine
   their eyes
Magical unicorns bear ladies on their backs,
The ladies close their musing eyes. No prophecies,
Remembered out of Babylonian almanacs,
Have closed the ladies' eyes, their minds are but
   a pool
Where even longing drowns under its own excess;
Nothing but stillness can remain when hearts are full
Of their own sweetness, bodies of their loveliness.

The cloud-pale unicorns, the eyes of aquamarine,
The quivering half-closed eyelids, the rags of cloud or
   of lace,
Or eyes that rage has brightened, arms it has made lean
Give place to an indifferent multitude, give place
To brazen hawks. Nor self-delighting reverie
Nor hate of what's to come, nor pity for what's gone,
Nothing but grip of claw, and the eye's complacency
The innumerable clanging wings that have put out
   the moon.

I turn away and shut the door, and on the stair
Wonder how many times I could have proved
   my worth

In something that all others understand or share;
But oh, ambitious heart, had such a proof drawn forth
A company of friends, a conscience set at ease,
It had but made us pine the more. The abstract joy,
The half read wisdom of daemonic images,
Suffice the ageing man as once the growing boy.

AGAINST UNWORTHY PRAISE

Oh, heart, be at peace, because
Nor knave nor dolt can break
What's not for their applause,
Being for a woman's sake.
Enough if the work has seemed,
So did she your strength renew,
A dream that a lion had dreamed
Till the wilderness cried aloud,
A secret between you two,
Between the proud and the proud.

What, still, you would have their praise!
But here's a haughtier text,
The labyrinth of her days
That her own strangeness perplexed.
And how what her dreaming gave
Earned slander ingratitude
From self-same dolt and knave;
Ay, and worse wrong than these.
Yet she, singing upon her road,
Half lion, half child, is at peace.

LOVE, BEAUTY
& PASSION
·❇·

THE FALLING OF THE LEAVES

Autumn is over the long leaves that love us,
And over the mice in the barley sheaves;
Yellow the leaves of the rowan above us,
And yellow the wet wild-strawberry leaves.

The hour of the waning of love has beset us,
And weary and worn are our sad souls now;
Let us part, ere the season of passion forget us,
With a kiss and a tear on thy drooping brow.

EPHEMERA

"Your eyes that once were never weary of mine
"Are bowed in sorrow under pendulous lids,
"Because our love is waning."

    And then she:
"Although our love is waning, let us stand
"By the lone border of the lake once more,
"Together in that hour of gentleness
"When the poor tired child, Passion, falls asleep:
"How far away the stars seem, and how far
"Is our first kiss, and ah, how old my heart!"

Pensive they paced along the faded leaves,
While slowly he whose hand held hers replied:
"Passion has often worn our wandering hearts."

The woods were round them, and the yellow leaves
Fell like faint meteors in the gloom, and once
A rabbit old and lame limped down the path;
Autumn was over him: and now they stood
On the lone border of the lake once more:
Turning, he saw that she had thrust dead leaves
Gathered in silence, dewy as her eyes,
In bosom and hair.

"Ah, do not mourn," he said,
"That we are tired, for other loves await us;
"Hate on and love through unrepining hours.
"Before us lies eternity; our souls
"Are love, and a continual farewell."

DOWN BY THE SALLEY GARDENS

Down by the salley gardens my love and I did meet;
She passed the salley gardens with little snow-
  white feet.
She bid me take love easy, as the leaves grow on
  the tree;
But I, being young and foolish, with her would
  not agree.

In a field by the river my love and I did stand,
And on my leaning shoulder she laid her snow-
  white hand.
She bid me take life easy, as the grass grows on
  the weirs;
But I was young and foolish, and now am full of tears.

THE ROSE OF THE WORLD

Who dreamed that beauty passes like a dream?
For these red lips, with all their mournful pride,
Mournful that no new wonder may betide,
Troy passed away in one high funeral gleam,
And Usna's children died.

We and the labouring world are passing by:
Amid men's souls, that waver and give place,
Like the pale waters in their wintry race,
Under the passing stars, foam of the sky,
Lives on this lonely face.

Bow down, archangels, in your dim abode:
Before you were, or any hearts to beat,
Weary and kind one lingered by His seat;
He made the world to be a grassy road
Before her wandering feet.

THE ROSE OF PEACE

If Michael, leader of God's host
When Heaven and Hell are met,
Looked down on you from Heaven's door-post
He would his deeds forget.

Brooding no more upon God's wars
In his Divine homestead,
He would go weave out of the stars
A chaplet for your head.

And all folk seeing him bow down,
And white stars tell your praise,
Would come at last to God's great town,
Led on by gentle ways;

And God would bid His warfare cease.
Saying all things were well;
And softly make a rosy peace,
A peace of Heaven with Hell.

THE PITY OF LOVE

A pity beyond all telling
Is hid in the heart of love:
The folk who are buying and selling
The clouds on their journey above
The cold wet winds ever blowing
And the shadowy hazel grove
Where mouse-gray waters are flowing
Threaten the head that I love.

THE SORROW OF LOVE

The quarrel of the sparrows in the eaves,
The full round moon and the star-laden sky,
And the loud song of the ever-singing leaves,
Had hid away earth's old and weary cry.

And then you came with those red mournful lips,
And with you came the whole of the world's tears
And all the trouble of her labouring ships,
And all the trouble of her myriad years.

And now the sparrows warring in the eaves,
The curd-pale moon, the white stars in the sky,
And the loud chaunting of the unquiet leaves,
Are shaken with earth's old and weary cry.

WHEN YOU ARE OLD

When you are old and gray and full of sleep,
And nodding by the fire, take down this book,
And slowly read, and dream of the soft look
Your eyes had once, and of their shadows deep;

How many loved your moments of glad grace,
And loved your beauty will love false or true;
But one man loved the pilgrim soul in you,
And loved the sorrows of your changing face.

And bending down beside the glowing bars
Murmur, a little sadly, how love fled
And paced upon the mountains overhead
And hid his face amid a crowd of stars.

THE WHITE BIRDS

I would that we were, my beloved, white birds on the
   foam of the sea!
We tire of the flame of the meteor, before it can fade
   and flee;
And the flame of the blue star of twilight, hung low on
   the rim of the sky,
Has awaked in our hearts, my beloved, a sadness that
   may not die.

A weariness comes from those dreamers, dew
   dabbled, the lily and rose;
Ah, dream not of them, my beloved, the flame of the
   meteor that goes,
Or the flame of the blue star that lingers hung low in
   the fall of the dew:
For I would we were changed to white birds on the
   wandering foam: I and you!

I am haunted by numberless islands, and many a
   Danaan shore,
Where Time would surely forget us, and Sorrow come
   near us no more;
Soon far from the rose and the lily, and fret of the
   flames would we be,
Were we only white birds, my beloved, buoyed out on
   the foam of the sea!

A CRADLE SONG

"Coth yani me von gilli beg,
"'N beur ve thu more a creena."

The angels are stooping
Above your bed;
They weary of trooping
With the whimpering dead.

God's laughing in heaven
To see you so good;
The Shining Seven
Are gay with His mood.

I kiss you and kiss you,
My pigeon, my own;
Ah, how I shall miss you
When you have grown.

AEDH TELLS OF THE ROSE IN
HIS HEART

All things uncomely and broken, all things worn out
    and old,
The cry of a child by the roadway, the creak of a
    lumbering cart,
The heavy steps of the ploughman, splashing the
    wintry mould,
Are wronging your image that blossoms a rose in the
    deeps of my heart.

The wrong of unshapely things is a wrong too great to
    be told;
I hunger to build them anew and sit on a green
    knoll apart,
With the earth and the sky and the water, remade, like
    a casket of gold
For my dreams of your image that blossoms a rose in
    the deeps of my heart.

THE HEART OF THE WOMAN

O what to me the little room
That was brimmed up with prayer and rest;
He bade me out into the gloom,
And my breast lies upon his breast

O what to me my mother's care,
The house where I was safe and warm;
The shadowy blossom of my hair
Will hide us from the bitter storm.

O hiding hair and dewy eyes,
I am no more with life and death,
My heart upon his warm heart lies,
My breath is mixed into his breath.

AEDH LAMENTS THE LOSS OF LOVE

Pale brows, still hands and dim hair,
I had a beautiful friend
And dreamed that the old despair
Would end in love in the end:
She looked in my heart one day
And saw your image was there;
She has gone weeping away.

MICHAEL ROBARTES BIDS HIS BELOVED BE AT PEACE

I hear the Shadowy Horses, their long manes a-shake,
Their hoofs heavy with tumult, their eyes
    glimmering white;
The North unfolds above them clinging,
    creeping night,
The East her hidden joy before the morning break,
The West weeps in pale dew and sighs passing away,
The South is pouring down roses of crimson fire:
O vanity of Sleep, Hope, Dream, endless Desire,
The Horses of Disaster plunge in the heavy clay:
Beloved, let your eyes half close, and your heart beat
Over my heart, and your hair fall over my breast,
Drowning love's lonely hour in deep twilight of rest,
And hiding their tossing manes and their
    tumultuous feet.

HANRAHAN REPROVES THE CURLEW

O, curlew, cry no more in the air,
Or only to the waters in the West;
Because your crying brings to my mind
Passion-dimmed eyes and long heavy hair
That was shaken out over my breast:
There is enough evil in the crying of wind.

A POET TO HIS BELOVED

I bring you with reverent hands
The books of my numberless dreams;
White woman that passion has worn
As the tide wears the dove-gray sands,
And with heart more old than the horn
That is brimmed from the pale fire of time:
White woman with numberless dreams
I bring you my passionate rhyme.

AEDH GIVES HIS BELOVED
CERTAIN RHYMES

Fasten your hair with a golden pin,
And bind up every wandering tress;
I bade my heart build these poor rhymes:
It worked at them, day out, day in,
Building a sorrowful loveliness
Out of the battles of old times.

You need but lift a pearl-pale hand,
And bind up your long hair and sigh;
And all men's hearts must burn and heat;
And candle-like foam on the dim sand,
And stars climbing the dew-dropping sky,
Live but to light your passing feet.

AEDH WISHES HIS BELOVED WERE DEAD

Were you but lying cold and dead,
And lights were paling out of the West,
You would come hither, and bend your head,
And I would lay my head on your breast;
And you would murmur tender words,
Forgiving me, because you were dead:
Nor would you rise and hasten away,
Though you have the will of the wild birds,
But know your hair was bound and wound
About the stars and moon and sun:
O would beloved that you lay
Under the dock-leaves in the ground,
While lights were paling one by one.

AEDH WISHES FOR THE CLOTHS OF HEAVEN

Had I the heavens' embroidered cloths,
Enwrought with golden and silver light,
The blue and the dim and the dark cloths
Of night and light and the half light,
I would spread the cloths under your feet:
But I, being poor, have only my dreams;
I have spread my dreams under your feet;
Tread softly because you tread on my dreams.

THE ARROW

I thought of your beauty and this arrow
Made out of a wild thought is in my marrow.
There's no man may look upon her, no man,
As when newly grown to be a woman,
Blossom pale, she pulled down the pale blossom
At the moth hour and hid it in her bosom.
This beauty's kinder yet for a reason
I could weep that the old is out of season.

THE FOLLY OF BEING COMFORTED

One that is ever kind said yesterday:
"Your well beloved's hair has threads of grey
And little shadows come about her eyes;
Time can but make it easier to be wise
Though now it's hard, till trouble is at an end;
And so be patient, be wise and patient friend".
But heart, there is no comfort, not a grain
Time can but make her beauty over again
Because of that great nobleness of hers;
The fire that stirs about her, when she stirs
Burns but more clearly; O she had not these ways,
When all the wild summer was in her gaze.
O heart O heart if she'd but turn her head,
You'd know the folly of being comforted.

OLD MEMORY

I thought to fly to her when the end of day
Awakens an old memory, and say,
"Your strength, that is so lofty and fierce and kind,
It might call up a new age, calling to mind
The queens that were imagined long ago,
Is but half yours: he kneaded in the dough
Through the long years of youth, and who would
    have thought
It all, and more than it all, would come to naught,
And that dear words meant nothing?" But enough,
For when we have blamed the wind we can
    blame love;
Or, if there needs be more, be nothing said
That would be harsh for children that have strayed.

NEVER GIVE ALL THE HEART

Never give all the heart, for love
Will hardly seem worth thinking of
To passionate women if it seem
Certain, and they never dream
That it fades out from kiss to kiss;
For everything that's lovely is
But a brief dreamy kind delight.
O never give the heart outright,
For they, for all smooth lips can say,
Have given their hearts up to the play.
And who could play it well enough
If deaf and dumb and blind with love?
He that made this knows all the cost,
For he gave all his heart and lost.

THE HOLLOW WOOD

O hurry to the water amid the trees,
For there the tall deer and his leman sigh
When they have but looked upon their images,
O that none ever loved but you and I!

Or have you heard that sliding silver-shoed,
Pale silver-proud queen-woman of the sky,
When the sun looked out of his golden hood,
O that none ever loved but you and I!

O hurry to the hollow wood, for there
I will drive out the deer and moon and cry –
O my share of the world, O yellow hair,
No one has ever loved but you and I!

O DO NOT LOVE TOO LONG

Sweetheart, do not love too long:
I loved long and long,
And grew to be out of fashion
Like an old song.
All through the years of our youth
Neither could have known
Their own thought from the other's,
We were so much at one.
But, O in a minute she changed –
O do not love too long,
Or you will grow out of fashion
Like an old song.

A WOMAN HOMER SUNG

If any man drew near
When I was young,
I thought "he holds her dear"
And shook with hate and fear.
But oh, 'twas bitter wrong.
If he could pass her by
With an indifferent eye.

Whereon I wrote and wrought
And now being grey,
I dream that I have brought
To such a pitch my thought
That coming time can say,
"He shadowed in a glass
What thing her body was."

For she had fiery blood
When I was young.
And trod so sweetly proud
As 'twere upon a cloud,
A woman Homer sung.
That life and letters seem
But an heroic dream.

RECONCILIATION

Some may have blamed you that you took away
The verses that they cared for on the day
When, the ears being deafened, the sight of the
    eyes blind
With lightning you went from me, and I could find
Nothing to make a song about but kings,
Helmets, and swords, and half-forgotten things
That were like memories of you – but now
We'll out for the world lives as long ago;
And while we're in our laughing, weeping fit.
Hurl helmets, crowns, and swords into the pit.
But, dear, cling close to me; since you were gone,
My barren thoughts have chilled me to the bone.

KING AND NO KING

"Would it were anything but merely voice"
The NO King cried who after that was King,
Because he had not heard of anything
That balanced with a word is more than noise;
Yet Old Romance being kind, let him prevail
Somewhere or somehow that I have forgot,
Though he'd but cannon – Whereas we that had thought
To have lit upon as clean and sweet a tale
Have been defeated by that pledge you gave
In momentary anger long ago;
And I that have not your faith, how shall I know
That in the blinding light beyond the grave
We'll find so good a thing as that we have lost?
The hourly kindness, the day's common speech,
The habitual content of each with each
When neither soul nor body has been crossed.

PEACE

Ah, that Time could touch a form
That could show what Homer's age
Bred to be a hero's wage.
"Were not all her life but storm,
Would not painters paint a form
Of such noble lines I said?
Such a delicate high head,
So much sternness and such charm."
Ah, but peace that comes at length,
Came when Time had touched her form.

A DRINKING SONG

Wine comes in at the mouth
And love comes in at the eye;
That's all we shall know for truth
Before we grow old and die.
I lift the glass to my mouth,
I look at you, and I sigh.

A LYRIC FROM AN UNPUBLISHED PLAY

"Put off that mask of burning gold
With emerald eyes."
"O no, my dear, you make so bold
To find if hearts be wild and wise,
And yet not cold."

"I would but find what's there to find,
Love or deceit."
"It was the mask engaged your mind,
And after set your heart to beat,
Not what's behind."

"But lest you are my enemy,
I must enquire."
"O no, my dear, let all that be,
What matter, so there is but fire
In you, in me?"

THE YOUNG MAN'S SONG

I whispered "I am too young,"
And then, "I am old enough,"
Wherefore I threw a penny
To find out if I might love;
"Go and love, go and love young man,
If the lady be young and fair,"
Ah, penny, brown penny, brown penny,
I am looped in the loops of her hair.

Oh love is the crooked thing,
There is nobody wise enough
To find out all that is in it,
For he would be thinking of love
Till the stars had run away,
And the shadows eaten the moon;
Ah penny, brown penny, brown penny,
One cannot begin it too soon.

A FRIEND'S ILLNESS

Sickness brought me this
Thought, in that scale of his:
Why should I be dismayed
Though flame had burned the whole
World, as it were a coal,
Now I have seen it weighed
Against a soul?

WHEN HELEN LIVED

We have cried in our despair
That men desert,
For some trivial affair
Or noisy, insolent sport,
Beauty that we have won
From bitterest hours;
Yet we, had we walked within
Those topless towers
Where Helen walked with her boy,
Had given but as the rest
Of the men and women of Troy,
A word and a jest.

FALLEN MAJESTY

Although crowds gathered once if she but showed
   her face,
And even old men's eyes grew dim, this hand alone,
Like some last courtier at a gypsy camping place,
Babbling of fallen majesty, records what's gone.

The lineaments, a heart that laughter has made sweet,
These, these remain, but I record what's gone. A crowd
Will gather, and not know it walks the very street
Whereon a thing once walked that seemed a
   burning cloud.

FRIENDS

Now must I these three praise –
Three women that have wrought
What joy is in my days;
One that no passing thought,
Nor those unpassing cares,
No, not in these fifteen
Many times troubled years,
Could ever come between
Heart and delighted heart;
And one because her hand
Had strength that could unbind
What none can understand,
What none can have and thrive,
Youth's dreamy load, till she
So changed me that I live
Labouring in ecstasy.
And what of her that took
All till my youth was gone
With scarce a pitying look?
How should I praise that one?
When day begins to break
I count my good and bad,
Being wakeful for her sake,
Remembering what she had,
What eagle look still shows,
While up from my heart's root
So great a sweetness flows
I shake from head to foot.

THAT THE NIGHT COME

She lived in storm and strife,
Her soul had such desire
For what proud death may bring
That it could not endure
The common good of life,
But lived as 'twere a king
That packed his marriage day
With banneret and pennon,
Trumpet and kettledrum,
And the outrageous cannon,
To bundle time away
That the night come.

ON WOMAN

May God be praised for woman
That gives up all her mind,
A man may find in no man
A friendship of her kind
That covers all he has brought
As with her flesh and bone
Nor quarrels with a thought
Because it is not her own.

Though pedantry denies
It's plain The Bible means
That Solomon grew wise
While talking with his queens
Yet never could, although
They say he counted grass,
Count all the praises due
When Sheba was his lass,
When she the iron wrought, or
When from the smithy fire
It shuddered in the water:
Harshness of their desire
That made them stretch and yawn,
Pleasure that comes with sleep,
Shudder that made them one.
What else he give or keep
God grant me – no not here,

For I am not so bold
To hope a thing so dear
Now I am growing old.
But when if the tale's true
The Pestle of the moon
That pounds up all anew
Brings me to birth again –
To find what once I had
And know what once I have known,
Until I am driven mad,
Sleep driven from my bed,
By tenderness and care,
Pity, an aching head,
Gnashing of teeth, despair;
And all because of some one
Perverse creature of chance,
And live like Solomon
That Sheba led a dance.

HER PRAISE

She is foremost of those that I would hear praised.
I have gone about the house, gone up and down
As a man does who has published a new book
Or a young girl dressed out in her new gown,
And though I have turned the talk by hook or crook
Until her praise should be the uppermost theme,
A woman spoke of some new tale she had read;
A man so vaguely that he seemed to dream
Of some strange woman's name that ran in his head.

She is foremost of those that I would hear praised.
I will talk no more of books or the long war
But walk by the dry thorn until I have found
Some beggar sheltering from the wind, and there
Manage the talk until her name come round.
If there be rags enough he will know her name
And be well pleased remembering it, for in the
    old days,
Though she had young men's praise and old
    men's blame,
Among the poor both old and young gave her praise.

HIS PHOENIX

There is a queen in China, or may be it's in Spain,
And birthdays and holidays such praises can be heard
Of her unblemished lineaments, a whiteness with
   no stain,
That she might be that sprightly girl who was
   trodden by a bird;
And there's a score of duchesses, surpassing
   woman-kind,
Or who have found a painter to make them so for pay
And smooth out stain and blemish with the elegance
   of his mind:
I knew a phoenix in my youth so let them have their day.

The young men every night applaud their Gaby's
   laughing eye,
And Ruth St Denis had more charm although she had
   poor luck,
From nineteen hundred nine or ten, Pavlova's had
   the cry,
And there's a player in The States who gathers up
   her cloak
And flings herself out of the room when Juliet would
   be bride
With all a woman's passion, a child's imperious way,
And there are – but no matter if there are scores beside:
I knew a phoenix in my youth so let them have their day.

There's Margaret and Marjorie and Dorothy and Nan,
A Daphne and a Mary who live in privacy;
One's had her fill of lovers, another's had but one,
Another boasts "I pick and choose and have but two
   or three."
If head and limb have beauty and the instep's high
   and light
They can spread out what sail they please for all I have
   to say,
Be but the breakers of men's hearts or engines of
   delight:
I knew a phoenix in my youth so let them have their day.

There'll be that crowd to make men wild through all
   the centuries,
And may be there'll be some young belle walk out to
   make men wild
Who is my beauty's equal, though that my
   heart denies,
But not the exact likeness, the simplicity of a child,
And that proud look as though she had gazed into the
   burning sun,
And all the shapely body no tittle gone astray,
I mourn for that most lonely thing; and yet God's will
   be done,
I knew a phoenix in my youth so let them have their day.

A THOUGHT FROM PROPERTIUS

She might, so noble from head
To great shapely knees
The long flowing line,
Have walked to the altar
Through the holy images
At Pallas Athene's side,
Or been fit spoil for a centaur
Drunk with the un-mixed wine.

BROKEN DREAMS

There is gray in your hair.
Young men no longer suddenly catch their breath
When you are passing;
But maybe some old gaffer mutters a blessing
Because it was your prayer
Recovered him upon the bed of death.
But for your sake – that all heart's ache have known,
And given to others all heart's ache,
From meagre girlhood's putting on
Burdensome beauty – but for your sake
Heaven has put away the stroke of her doom,
So great her portion in that peace you make
By merely walking in a room.

Your beauty can but leave among us
Vague memories, nothing but memories.
A young man when the old men are done talking
Will say to an old man, "Tell me of that lady
The poet stubborn with his passion sang us
When age might well have chilled his blood."

Vague memories, nothing but memories,
But in the grave all, all, shall be renewed.
The certainty that I shall see that lady
Leaning or standing or walking
In the first loveliness of womanhood,

And with the fervour of my youthful eyes,
Has set me muttering like a fool.
You are more beautiful than anyone
And yet your body had a flaw:
Your small hands were not beautiful.
And I am afraid that you will run
And paddle to the wrist
In that mysterious, always brimming lake
Where those that have obeyed the holy law
Paddle and are perfect; leave unchanged
The hands that I have kissed
For old sakes' sake.

The last stroke of midnight dies.
All day in the one chair
From dream to dream and rhyme to rhyme I
    have ranged
In rambling talk with an image of air:
Vague memories, nothing but memories.

A DEEP-SWORN VOW

Others because you did not keep
That deep-sworn vow have been friends of mine;
Yet always when I look death in the face,
When I clamber to the heights of sleep,
Or when I grow excited with wine.
Suddenly I meet your face.

THE LOVER SPEAKS

A strange thing surely that my Heart when love had
    come unsought
Upon the northern upland or in that poplar shade,
Should find no burden but itself and yet should be
    worn out.
It could not bear that burden and therefore it
    went mad.

The south wind brought it longing, and the east
    wind despair,
The west wind made it pitiful, and the north
    wind afraid.
It feared to give its love a hurt with all the
    tempest there;
It feared the hurt that she could give and therefore it
    went mad.

I can exchange opinion with any neighbouring mind,
I have as healthy flesh and blood as any rhymer's had,
But oh my Heart could bear no more when the upland
    caught the wind;
I ran, I ran, from my love's side because my Heart
    went mad.

THE HEART REPLIES

The Heart behind its rib laughed out. "You have called
    me mad," it said.
"Because I made you turn away and run from that
    young child;
How could she mate with fifty years that was so
    wildly bred?
Let the cage bird and the cage bird mate and the wild
    bird mate in the wild."

"You but imagine lies all day, O murderer", I replied.
"And all those lies have but one end, poor wretches
    to betray;
I did not find in any cage the woman at my side.
O but her heart would break to learn my thoughts are
    far away."

"Speak all your mind" my Heart sang out, "speak all
    your mind; who cares,
Now that your tongue cannot persuade the child till
    she mistake
Her childish gratitude for love and match your
    fifty years.
O let her choose a young man now and all for his
    wild sake."

UNDER SATURN

Do not because this day I have grown saturnine
Imagine that some lost love, unassailable
Being a portion of my youth, can make me pine
And so forget the comfort that no words can tell
Your coming brought; though I acknowledge that I
    have gone
On a fantastic ride, my horse's flanks were spurred
By childish memories of an old cross Pollexfen,
And of a Middleton, whose name you never heard,
And of a red-haired Yeats whose looks, although
    he died
Before my time, seem like a vivid memory.
You heard that labouring man who had served my
    people. He said
Upon the open road, near to the Sligo quay –
No, no, not said, but cried it out – "You have
    come again
And surely after twenty years it was time to come."
I am thinking of a child's vow sworn in vain
Never to leave that valley his fathers called their home.

LIFE, AGE & DEATH

THE MEDITATION OF THE
OLD FISHERMAN

You waves, though you dance by my feet like children
    at play,
Though you glow and you glance, though you purr
    and you dart;
In the Junes that were warmer than these are, the
    waves were more gay,
When I was a boy with never a crack in my heart.

The herring are not in the tides as they were of old;
My sorrow! for many a creak gave the creel in the cart
That carried the take to Sligo town to be sold,
When I was a boy with never a crack in my heart.

And ah, you proud maiden, you are not so fair when
    his oar
Is heard on the water, as they were, the proud
    and apart,
Who paced in the eve by the nets on the pebbly shore,
When I was a boy with never a crack in my heart.

THE BALLAD OF MOLL MAGEE

Come round me, little childer;
There, don't fling stones at me
Because I mutter as I go;
But pity Moll Magee.

My man was a poor fisher
With shore lines in the say;
My work was saltin' herrings
The whole of the long day.

And sometimes from the saltin' shed,
I scarce could drag my feet
Under the blessed moonlight,
Along the pebbly street.

I'd always been but weakly,
And my baby was just born;
A neighbour minded her by day
I minded her till morn.

I lay upon my baby;
Ye little childer dear,
I looked on my cold baby
When the morn grew frosty and clear.

A weary woman sleeps so hard!
My man grew red and pale,
And gave me money, and bade me go
To my own place, Kinsale.

He drove me out and shut the door,
And gave his curse to me;
I went away in silence,
No neighbour could I see.

The windows and the doors were shut,
One star shone faint and green
The little straws were turnin' round
Across the bare boreen.

I went away in silence:
Beyond old Martin's byre
I saw a kindly neighbour
Blowin' her mornin' fire.

She drew from me my story –
My money's all used up,
And still, with pityin', scornin' eye,
She gives me bite and sup.

She says my man will surely come,
And fetch me home agin;
But always, as I'm movin' round,
Without doors or within,

Pilin' the wood or pilin' the turf,
Or goin' to the well,
I'm thinkin' of my baby
And keenin' to mysel'.

And sometimes I am sure she knows
When, openin' wide His door,
God lights the stars, His candles,
And looks upon the poor.

So now, ye little childer,
Ye won't fling stones at me;
But gather with your shinin' looks
And pity Moll Magee.

THE BALLAD OF THE FOXHUNTER

"Now lay me in a cushioned chair
"And carry me, you four,
"With cushions here and cushions there,
"To see the world once more.

"And some one from the stables bring
"My Dermot dear and brown,
"And lead him gently in a ring,
"And gently up and down.

"Now leave the chair upon the grass:
"Bring hound and huntsman here,
"And I on this strange road will pass,
"Filled full of ancient cheer."

His eyelids droop, his head falls low,
His old eyes cloud with dreams;
The sun upon all things that grow
Pours round in sleepy streams.

Brown Dermot treads upon the lawn,
And to the armchair goes,
And now the old man's dreams are gone,
He smooths the long brown nose.

And now moves many a pleasant tongue
Upon his wasted hands,
For leading aged hounds and young
The huntsman near him stands.

"My huntsman, Rody, blow the horn,
"And make the hills reply."
The huntsman loosens on the morn
A gay and wandering cry.

A fire is in the old man's eyes,
His fingers move and sway,
And when the wandering music dies
They hear him feebly say,

"My huntsman, Rody, blow the horn,
"And make the hills reply."
"I cannot blow upon my horn,
"I can but weep and sigh."

The servants round his cushioned place
Are with new sorrow wrung;
And hounds are gazing on his face,
Both aged hounds and young.

One blind hound only lies apart
On the sun-smitten grass;
He holds deep commune with his heart:
The moments pass and pass;

The blind hound with a mournful din
Lifts slow his wintry head;
The servants bear the body in;
The hounds wail for the dead.

A DREAM OF DEATH

I dreamed that one had died in a strange place
Near no accustomed hand;
And they had nailed the boards above her face
The peasants of that land,
Wondering to lay her in that solitude,
And raised above her mound
A cross they had made out of two bits of wood,
And planted cypress round;
And left her to the indifferent stars above
Until I carved these words:
She was more beautiful than thy first love,
But now lies under boards.

THE LAMENTATION OF THE OLD PENSIONER

I had a chair at every hearth,
When no one turned to see,
With "Look at that old fellow there,
"And who may he be?"
And therefore do I wander now,
And the fret lies on me.

The road-side trees keep murmuring
Ah, wherefore murmur ye,
As in the old days long gone by,
Green oak and poplar tree?
The well-known faces are all gone
And the fret lies on me.

THE HOST OF THE AIR

O'Driscoll drove with a song
The wild duck and the drake
From the tall and the tufted reeds
Of the drear Hart Lake.

And he saw how the reeds grew dark
At the coming of night tide,
And dreamed of the long dim hair
Of Bridget his bride.

He heard while he sang and dreamed
A piper piping away,
And never was piping so sad,
And never was piping so gay.

And he saw young men and young girls
Who danced on a level place
And Bridget his bride among them,
With a sad and a gay face.

The dancers crowded about him,
And many a sweet thing said,
And a young man brought him red wine
And a young girl white bread.

But Bridget drew him by the sleeve,
Away from the merry bands,

To old men playing at cards
With a twinkling of ancient hands.

The bread and the wine had a doom,
For these were the host of the air;
He sat and played in a dream
Of her long dim hair.

He played with the merry old men
And thought not of evil chance,
Until one bore Bridget his bride
Away from the merry dance.

He bore her away in his arms,
The handsomest young man there,
And his neck and his breast and his arms
Were drowned in her long dim hair.

O'Driscoll scattered the cards
And out of his dream awoke:
Old men and young men and young girls
Were gone like a drifting smoke;

But he heard high up in the air
A piper piping away,
And never was piping so sad,
And never was piping so gay.

THE SONG OF THE OLD MOTHER

I rise in the dawn, and I kneel and blow
Till the seed of the fire flicker and glow;
And then I must scrub and bake and sweep
Till stars are beginning to blink and peep;
And the young lie long and dream in their bed
Of the matching of ribbons for bosom and head,
And their day goes over in idleness,
And they sigh if the wind but lift a tress:
While I must work because I am old,
And the seed of the fire gets feeble and cold.

THE POET PLEADS WITH HIS FRIEND FOR OLD FRIENDS

Though you are in your shining days,
Voices among the crowd
And new friends busy with your praise,
Be not unkind or proud,
But think about old friends the most:
Time's bitter flood will rise,
Your beauty perish and be lost
For all eyes but these eyes.

THE OLD MEN ADMIRING THEMSELVES IN THE WATER

I heard the old, old men say
"Everything alters,
And one by one we drop away".
They had hands like claws, and their knees
Were twisted like the old thorn trees
By the waters.
I heard the old old men say
"All that's beautiful drifts away
Like the waters."

THE COMING OF WISDOM WITH TIME

Though leaves are many, the root is one;
Through all the lying days of my youth
I swayed my leaves and flowers in the sun;
Now I may wither into the truth.

THE THREE HERMITS

Three old hermits took the air
By a cold and desolate sea,
First was muttering a prayer,
Second rummaged for a flea;
On a windy stone, the third,
Giddy with his hundredth year,
Sang unnoticed like a bird.
"Though the Door of Death is near
And what waits behind the door,
Three times in a single day
I, though upright on the shore,
Fall asleep when I should pray."
So the first but now the second,
"We're but given what we have earned
When all thoughts and deeds are reckoned,
So it's plain to be discerned
That the shades of holy men,
Who have failed being weak of will,
Pass the Door of Birth again,
And are plagued by crowds, until
They've the passion to escape."
Moaned the other "They are thrown
Into some most fearful shape."
But the second mocked his moan:
"They are not changed to anything,
Having loved God once, but maybe,

To a poet or a king
Or a witty lovely lady."
While he'd rummaged rags and hair,
Caught and cracked his flea, the third,
Giddy with his hundredth year
Sang unnoticed like a bird.

BEGGAR TO BEGGAR CRIED

"Time to put off the world and go somewhere
And find my health again in the sea air,"
Beggar to beggar cried, being frenzy-struck,
"And make my soul before my pate is bare."

"And get a comfortable wife and house
To rid me of the devil in my shoes,"
Beggar to beggar cried, being frenzy-struck,
"And the worse devil that is between my thighs."

"And though I'd marry with a comely lass,
She need not be too comely – let it pass,"
Beggar to beggar cried, being frenzy-struck,
"But there's a devil in a looking-glass."

"Nor should she be too rich, because the rich
Are driven by wealth as beggars by the itch,"
Beggar to beggar cried, being frenzy-struck,
"And cannot have a humorous happy speech."

"And there I'll grow respected at my ease,
And hear amid the garden's nightly peace,"
Beggar to beggar cried, being frenzy-struck,
"The wind-blown clamour of the barnacle-geese."

RUNNING TO PARADISE

As I came over Windy Gap
They threw a halfpenny into my cap
For I am running to Paradise.
And all that I need do is to wish
And somebody puts his hand in the dish
To throw me a bit of salted fish
And there the king *is* but as the beggar.

My brother Mourteen is worn out
With skelping his big brawling lout,
And I am running to Paradise.
A poor life do what he can,
And though we keep a dog and a gun,
A serving maid and a serving man,
And there the king *is* but as the beggar.

Poor men have grown to be rich men,
And rich men grown to be poor again,
While I am running to Paradise.
And many a darling wit's grown dull
That tossed a bare heel when at school,
Now it has filled an old sock full,
And there the king *is* but as the beggar.

The wind is old and still at play
While I must hurry upon my way
For I am running to Paradise.
Yet never have I lit on a friend
To take my fancy like the wind
That nobody can buy or bind
And there the king *is* but as the beggar.

THE PLAYER QUEEN
(Song from an Unfinished Play)

My mother dandled me and sang,
"How young it is, how young!"
And made a golden cradle
That on a willow swung.

"He went away," my mother sang,
"When I was brought to bed,"
And all the while her needle pulled
The gold and silver thread.

She pulled the thread and bit the thread
And made a golden gown,
And wept because she had dreamt that I
Was born to wear a crown.

"When she was got," my mother sang,
"I heard a sea-mew cry,
And saw a flake of the yellow foam
That dropped upon my thigh."

How therefore could she help but braid
The gold into my hair,
And dream that I should carry
The golden top of care?

TO A CHILD DANCING IN THE WIND

I

Dance there upon the shore;
What need have you to care
For wind or water's roar?
And tumble out your hair
That the salt drops have wet;
Being young you have not known
The fool's triumph, nor yet
Love lost as soon as won,
Nor the best labourer dead
And all the sheaves to bind.
What need have you to dread
The monstrous crying of wind?

II

Has no one said those daring
Kind eyes should be more learn'd?
I have found out how despairing
The moths are when they are burned,
But I am old and you are young
So we speak a different tongue.

O you will take whatever's offered
And dream that all the world's a friend,
Suffer as your mother suffered,
Be as broken in the end.
I could have warned you – but you are young,
And I speak a barbarous tongue.

A MEMORY OF YOUTH

The moments passed as at a play,
I had the wisdom love brings forth;
I had my share of mother wit
And yet for all that I could say,
And though I had her praise for it,
A cloud blown from the cut-throat north
Suddenly hid love's moon away.

Believing every word I said
I praised her body and her mind
Till pride had made her eyes grow bright,
And pleasure made her cheeks grow red,
And vanity her footfall light,
Yet we, for all that praise, could find
Nothing but darkness overhead.

We sat as silent as a stone,
We knew, though she'd not said a word,
That even the best of love must die,
And had been savagely undone
Were it not that love upon the cry
Of a most ridiculous little bird
Tore from the clouds his marvellous moon.

THE WILD SWANS AT COOLE

The trees are in their autumn beauty,
The woodland paths are dry,
Under the October twilight the water
Mirrors a still sky;
Upon the brimming water among the stones
Are nine and fifty swans.

The nineteenth Autumn has come upon me
Since I first made my count.
I saw, before I had well finished,
All suddenly mount
And scatter wheeling in great broken rings
Upon their clamorous wings.

I have looked upon those brilliant creatures,
And now my heart is sore.
All's changed since I, hearing at twilight,
The first time on this shore,
The bell-beat of their wings above my head,
Trod with a lighter tread.

Unwearied still, lover by lover,
They paddle in the cold,
Companionable streams or climb the air;
Their hearts have not grown old;
Passion or conquest, wander where they will,
Attend upon them still.

But now they drift on the still water
Mysterious, beautiful;
Among what rushes will they build,
By what lake's edge or pool
Delight men's eyes when I awake some day
To find they have flown away?

MEN IMPROVE WITH THE YEARS

I am worn out with dreams;
A weather-worn, marble triton
Among the streams;
And all day long I look
Upon this lady's beauty
As though I had found in book
A pictured beauty,
Pleased to have filled the eyes
Or the discerning ears,
Delighted to be but wise,
For men improve with the years
And yet and yet
Is this my dream, or the truth?
O would that we had met
When I had my burning youth;
But I grow old among dreams,
A weather-worn, marble triton
Among the streams.

MEMORY

One had a lovely face,
And two or three had charm,
But charm and face were in vain
Because the mountain grass
Cannot but keep the form
Where the mountain hare has lain.

IN MEMORY

Five and twenty years have gone
Since old William Pollexfen
Laid his strong bones down in death
By his wife Elizabeth
In the grey stone tomb he made.
And after twenty years they laid
In that tomb by him and her,
His son George, the astrologer;
And Masons drove from miles away
To scatter the Acacia spray
Upon a melancholy man
Who had ended where his breath began.

Many a son and daughter lies
Far from the customary skies,
The Mall and Eades's grammar school,
In London or in Liverpool;
But where is laid the sailor John?
That so many lands had known:
Quiet lands or unquiet seas
Where the Indians trade or Japanese.
He never found his rest ashore
Moping for one voyage more.
Where have they laid the sailor John?

And yesterday the youngest son,
A humorous, unambitious man.
Was buried near the astrologer;
And are we now in the tenth year?
Since he, who had been contented long,
A nobody in a great throng,
Decided he would journey home,
Now that his fiftieth year had come.
And "Mr. Alfred" be again
Upon the lips of common men
Who carried in their memory
His childhood and his family.

At all these death-beds women heard
A visionary white sea-bird
Lamenting that a man should die;
And with that cry I have raised my cry.

UPON A DYING LADY

I — *Her Courtesy*

With the old kindness, the old distinguished grace
She lies, her lovely piteous head amid dull red hair
Propped upon pillows, rouge on the pallor of her face.
She would not have us sad because she is lying there,
And when she meets our gaze her eyes are laughter-lit,
Her speech a wicked tale that we may vie with her
Matching our broken-hearted wit against her wit,
Thinking of saints and of Petronius Arbiter.

II — *Certain Artists Bring Her Dolls and Drawings*

Bring where our Beauty lies
A new modelled doll, or drawing,
With a friend's or an enemy's
Features, or may be showing
Her features when a tress
Of dull red hair was flowing
Over some silken dress
Cut in the Turkish fashion,
Or it maybe like a boy's.
We have given the world our passion
We have naught for death but toys.

III — *She Turns the Dolls' Faces to the Wall*

Because to-day is some religious festival
They had a priest say Mass, and even the Japanese,
Heel up and weight on toe, must face the wall
 – Pedant in passion, learned in old courtesies,
Vehement and witty she had seemed – the
      Venetian lady
Who had seemed to glide to some intrigue in her
      red shoes,
Her domino, her panniered skirt copied from Longhi;
The meditative critic; all are on their toes
Even our Beauty with her Turkish trousers on.
Because the priest must have like every dog his day
Or keep us all awake with baying at the moon,
We and our dolls being but the world were best away.

IV — *The End of Day*

She is playing like a child
And penance is the play,
Fantastical and wild
Because the end of day
Shows her that someone soon
Will come from the house, and say –
Though play is but half done –
"Come in and leave the play."

V — *Her Race*

She has not grown uncivil
As narrow natures would
And called the pleasures evil
Happier days thought good;
She knows herself a woman
No red and white of a face,
Or rank, raised from a common
Unreckonable race;
And how should her heart fail her
Or sickness break her will
With her dead brother's valour
For an example still.

VI — *Her Courage*

When her soul flies to the predestined dancing-place
(I have no speech but symbol, the pagan speech I made
Amid the dreams of youth) let her come face to face,
While wondering still to be a shade, with Grania's shade
All but the perils of the woodland flight forgot
That made her Dermuid dear, and some old cardinal
Pacing with half-closed eyelids in a sunny spot
Who had murmured of Giorgione at his latest breath –
Aye and Achilles, Timor, Babar, Barhaim all
Who have lived in joy and laughed into the face
    of Death.

VII — *Her Friends Bring Her a Christmas Tree*

Pardon great enemy,
Without an angry thought
We've carried in our tree,
And here and there have bought
Till all the boughs are gay,
And she may look from the bed
On pretty things that may
Please a fantastic head.
Give her a little grace
What if a laughing eye
Have looked into your face –
It is about to die.

YOUTH AND AGE

Much did I rage when young,
Being by the World oppressed,
But now with flattering tongue
It speeds the parting guest.

NOTES & INDEXES

YEATS ON HIS POEMS
Selected Notes

HERE FOLLOWS Yeats' own original notes on selected poems of his, following the order of the present collection.

The Ballad of Father Gilligan

A tradition among the people of Castleisland, Kerry.

The Hosting of the Sidhe

The powerful and wealthy called the gods of ancient Ireland the Tuatha De Danaan, or the Tribes of the goddess Danu, but the poor called them, and still sometimes call them, the Sidhe, from Aes Sidhe or Sluagh Sidhe, the people of the Faery Hills, as these words are usually explained. Sidhe is also Gaelic for wind, and certainly the Sidhe have much to do with the wind. They journey in whirling winds, winds that were called the dance of the daughters of Herodias in the Middle Ages, Herodias doubtless taking the place of some old goddess. When the country people see the leaves whirling on the road they bless themselves, because they believe the Sidhe to be passing by. They are almost always said to wear no covering upon their heads, and to let their hair stream out; and the great among them, for they have great and simple, go upon horseback. If any one becomes too much interested in them, and sees them over much, he loses all interest in ordinary things.

The Ballad of Father O'Hart

This ballad is founded on the story of a certain Father O'Hart, priest of Coloony, Sligo, in the last century, as told by the present priest of Coloony in his *History of Ballisodare and Kilvarnet*. The robbery of the lands of Father O'Hart was a kind of robbery which occurred but rarely during the penal laws. Catholics, forbidden to own landed property, evaded the law by giving a Protestant nominal possession of their estates. There are instances on record in which poor men were nominal owners of immense estates.

Down by the Salley Gardens

An extension of three lines sung to me by an old woman at Ballisodare.

The Meditation of the Old Fisherman

This poem is founded upon some things a fisherman said to me when out fishing in Sligo Bay.

The Ballad of the Foxhunter

Founded on an incident, probably itself a Tipperary tradition, in Kickham's *Knockagow*.

The Lamentation of the Old Pensioner

This poem is little more than a translation into verse of the very words of an old Wicklow peasant. Fret means doom or destiny.

The Host of the Air

Some writers distinguish between the Sluagh Gaoith, the host of the air, and Sluagh Sidhe, the host of the Sidhe, and describe the host of the air as of a peculiar malignancy. Dr. Joyce says, "of all the different kinds of goblins…air demons were most dreaded by the people. They lived among clouds, and mists, and rocks, and hated the human race with the utmost malignity" A very old Arann charm, which contains the words "Send God, by his strength, between us and the host of the Sidhe, between us and the host of the air," seems also to distinguish among them. I am inclined, however, to think that the distinction came in with Christianity and its belief about the prince of the air, for the host of the Sidhe, as I have already explained, are closely associated with the wind.

A Cradle Song; Michael Robartes Asks Forgiveness Because of His Many Moods

I use the wind as a symbol of vague desires and hopes, not merely because the Sidhe are in the wind, or because the wind bloweth as it listeth, but because wind and spirit and vague desire have been associated everywhere. A highland scholar tells me that in his country people use the wind in their talk and in their proverbs as I use it in my poem.

The Song of Wandering Aengus.

The Tribes of the goddess Danu can take all shapes, and those that are in the waters take often the shape of fish.

A woman of Burren, in Galway, says, "There are more of them in the sea than on the land, and they sometimes try to come over the side of the boat in the form of fishes, for they can take their choice shape." At other times they are beautiful women; and another Galway woman says, "Surely those things are in the sea as well as on land. My father was out fishing one night off Tyrone. And something came beside the boat that had eyes shining like candles. And then a wave came in, and a storm rose all in a minute, and whatever was in the wave, the weight of it had like to sink the boat. And then they saw that it was a woman in the sea that had the shining eyes. So my father went to the priest, and he bid him always to take a drop of holy water and a pinch of salt out in the boat with him, and nothing could harm him."

The poem was suggested to me by a Greek folk song; but the folk belief of Greece is very like that of Ireland, and I certainly thought, when I wrote it, of Ireland, and of the spirits that are in Ireland. An old man who was cutting a quickset hedge near Gort, in Galway, said, only the other day, "One time I was cutting timber over in Inchy, and about eight o'clock one morning, when I got there, I saw a girl picking nuts, with her hair hanging down over her shoulders; brown hair; and she had a good, clean face, and she was tall, and nothing on her head, and her dress no way gaudy, but simple. And when she felt me coming she gathered herself up, and was gone, as if the earth had swallowed her up. And I followed her, and looked for her, but I never could see her again from that day to this, never again."

The county Galway people use the word "clean" in its old sense of fresh and comely.

Michael Robartes Bids His Beloved Be at Peace

November, the old beginning of winter, or of the victory of the Fomor, or powers of death, and dismay, and cold, and darkness, is associated by the Irish people with the horse-shaped Pucas, who are now mischievous spirits, but were once Fomorian divinities. I think that they may have some connection with the horses of Mannannan, who reigned over the country of the dead, where the Fomorian Tethra reigned also; and the horses of Mannannan, though they could cross the land as easily as the sea, are constantly associated with the waves. Some neo-platonist, I forget who, describes the sea as a symbol of the drifting indefinite bitterness of life, and I believe there is like symbolism intended in the many Irish voyages to the islands of enchantment, or that there was, at any rate, in the mythology out of which these stories have been shaped. I follow much Irish and other mythology, and the magical tradition, in associating the North with night and sleep, and the East, the place of sunrise, with hope, and the South, the place of the sun when at its height, with passion and desire, and the West, the place of sunset, with fading and dreaming things.

Mongan Laments the Change that Has Come upon Him and His Beloved; Hanrahan Laments Because of His Wanderings

My deer and hound are properly related to the deer and hound that flicker in and out of the various tellings of the Arthurian legends, leading different knights upon adventures, and to the hounds and to the hornless deer at the beginning of, I think, all tellings of Oisín's journey to the country of the young. The hound is certainly related to the Hounds of Annwvyn or of Hades, who are white, and have red ears, and were heard, and are, perhaps, still heard by Welsh peasants following some flying thing in the night winds; and is probably related to the hounds that Irish country people believe will awake and seize the souls of the dead if you lament them too loudly or too soon, and to the hound the son of Setanta killed, on what was certainly, in the first form of the tale, a visit to the Celtic Hades. An old woman told a friend and myself that she saw what she thought were white birds, flying over an enchanted place, but found, when she got near, that they had dog's heads; and I do not doubt that my hound and these dog-headed birds are of the same family. I got my hound and deer out of a last century Gaelic poem about Oisín's journey to the country of the young. After the hunting of the hornless deer, that leads him to the seashore, and while he is riding over the sea with Niam, he sees amid the waters – I have not the Gaelic poem by me, and describe it from memory – a young man following a girl who has a golden apple, and afterwards a hound with one red ear following a deer with no horns. This hound and this deer seem plain images of the desire of man "which is for the woman", and "the desire of the woman which is for the desire of the man," and of all desires that are as these. I have read them in this way in "The Wanderings of Usheen" or Oisín, and have made my lover sigh because he has seen in their faces "the immortal desire of immortals." A solar mythologist would perhaps say that the girl with the golden apple was once the winter, or night, carrying the sun away, and the deer without horns, like the boar without bristles, darkness flying the light. He would certainly, I think, say that when Cuchullain, whom Professor Rhys calls a solar hero, hunted the enchanted deer of Slieve Fuadh, because the battle fury was still on him, he was the sun pursuing clouds, or cold, or darkness. I have understood them in this sense in "Hanrahan laments because of his wandering," and made Hanrahan long for the day when they, fragments of ancestral darkness, will overthrow the world. The desire of the woman, the flying darkness, it is all one! The image – across, a man preaching in the wilderness, a dancing Salome, a lily in a girl's hand, a flame leaping, a globe with wings, a pale sunset over still waters – is an eternal act; but our understandings are temporal and understand but a little at a time.

The man in my poem who has a hazel wand may have been Aengus, Master of Love; and I have made the boar without bristles come out of the West, because the place of sunset was in Ireland, as in other countries, a place of symbolic darkness and death.

The Cap and Bells

I dreamed this story exactly as I have written it, and dreamed another long dream after it, trying to make out its meaning, and whether I was to write it in prose or verse. The first dream was more a vision than a dream, for it was beautiful and coherent, and gave me the sense of illumination and exaltation that one gets from visions, while the second dream was confused and meaningless. The poem has always meant a great deal to me, though, as is the way with symbolic poems, it has not always meant quite the same thing. Blake would have said "the authors are in eternity," and I am quite sure they can only be questioned in dreams.

The Valley of the Black Pig

All over Ireland there are prophecies of the coming rout of the enemies of Ireland, in a certain Valley of the Black Pig, and these prophecies are, no doubt, now, as they were in the Fenian days, a political force. I have heard of one man who would not give any money to the Land League, because the Battle could not be until the close of the century; but, as a rule, periods of trouble bring prophecies of its near coming. A few years before my time, an old man who lived at Lisadell, in Sligo, used to fall down in a fit and rave out descriptions of the Battle; and a man in Sligo has told me that it will be so great a battle that the horses shall go up to their fetlocks in blood, and that their girths, when it is over, will rot from their bellies for lack of a hand to unbuckle them. The battle is a mythological battle, and the black pig is one with the bristleless boar, that killed Dearmod, in November, upon the western end of Ben Bulben; Misroide MacDatha's sow, whose carving brought on so great a battle; "the croppy black sow," and "the cutty black sow" of Welsh November rhymes ("Celtic Heathendom", pages 509–516); the boar that killed Adonis; the boar that killed Attis; and the pig embodiment of Typhon ("Golden Bough", II. pages 26, 31). The pig seems to have been originally a genius of the corn, and, seemingly because the too great power of their divinity makes divine things dangerous to mortals, its flesh was forbidden to many eastern nations; but as the meaning of the prohibition was forgotten, abhorrence took the place of reverence, pigs and boars grew into types of evil, and were described as the enemies of the very gods they once typified ("Golden Bough", 11. 26–31, 56–57). The Pig would, therefore, become the Black Pig, a type of cold and of winter that awake in November, the old beginning of winter, to do battle with the summer, and with the fruit and leaves, and finally, as I suggest; and as I believe, for the purposes of poetry; of the darkness that will at last destroy the gods and the world. The country people say there is no shape for a spirit to take so dangerous as the shape of a pig ; and a Galway black-smith – and blacksmiths are thought to be especially protected – says he would be afraid to meet a pig on the road at night; and another Galway man tells this story: "There was a man coming the road from Gort to Garryland one night, and he had a drop taken; and before him, on the road, he saw a pig walking; and having a drop in, he gave a shout, and made a kick at it, and bid it get out of that. And by the time he got home, his arm was swelled from the shoulder to be as big as a bag, and he couldn't use his hand with the pain of it. And his wife brought him, after a few days, to a woman that used to do cures at Rahasane. And on the road all she could do would hardly keep him from lying down to sleep on the grass. And when they got to the woman she knew all that happened; and, says she, it's well for you that your wife didn't let you fall asleep on the grass, for if you had done that but even for one instant, you'd be a lost man."

It is possible that bristles were associated with fertility, as the tail certainly was, for a pig's tail is stuck into the ground in Courland, that the corn may grow abundantly, and the tails of pigs, and other animal embodiments of the corn genius, are dragged over the ground to make it fertile in different countries. Professor Rhys, who considers the bristleless boar a symbol of darkness and cold, rather than of winter and cold, thinks it was without bristles because the darkness is shorn away by the sun. It may have had different meanings, just as the scourging of the man-god has had different though not contradictory meanings in different epochs of the world.

The Battle should, I believe, be compared with three other battles; a battle the Sidhe are said to fight when a person is being taken away by them; a battle they are said to fight in November for the harvest; the great battle the Tribes of the goddess Danu fought, according to the Gaelic chroniclers, with the Fomor at Moy Tura, or the Towery Plain.

I have heard of the battle over the dying both in County Galway and in the Isles of Arann, an old Arann fisherman having told me that it was fought over two of his children, and that he found blood in a box he had for keeping fish, when it was over; and I have written about it, and given examples elsewhere. A faery doctor, on the borders of Galway and Clare, explained it as a battle between the friends and enemies of the dying, the one party trying to take them, the other trying to save them from being taken. It may once, when the land of the Sidhe was the only other world, and when every man who died was carried thither, have always accompanied death. I suggest that the battle between the Tribes of the goddess Danu, the powers of light, and warmth, and fruitfulness, and goodness, and the Fomor, the powers of darkness, and cold, and barrenness, and badness upon the Towery Plain, was the establishment of the habitable world, the rout of the ancestral darkness; that the battle among the Sidhe for the harvest is the annual battle of summer and winter; that the battle among the Sidhe at a man's death is the battle of life and death; and that the battle of the Black Pig is the battle between the manifest world and the ancestral darkness at the end of all things; and that all these battles are one, the battle of all things with shadowy decay. Once a symbolism has possessed the imagination of large numbers of men, it becomes, as I believe, an embodiment of disembodied powers, and repeats itself in dreams and visions, age after age.

The Secret Rose

I find that I have unintentionally changed the old story of Conchobar's death. He did not see the crucifixion in a vision, but was told about it. He had been struck by a ball, made of the dried brain of a dead enemy, and hurled out of a sling; and this ball had been left in his head, and his head had been mended, the Book of Leinster says, with thread of gold because his hair was like gold. Keating, a writer of the time of Elizabeth, says, "In that state did he remain seven years, until the Friday on which Christ was crucified, according to some historians; and when he saw the unusual changes of the creation and the eclipse of the sun and the moon at its full, he asked of Bucrach, a Leinster Druid, who was along with him, what was it that brought that unusual change upon the planets of Heaven and Earth. "Jesus Christ, the son of God," said the Druid, "who is now being crucified by the Jews." "That is a pity," said Conchobar; "were I in his presence I would kill those who were putting him to death." And with that he brought out his sword, and rushed at a woody grove which was convenient to him, and began to cut and fell it; and what he said was, that if he were among the Jews that was the usage he would give them, and from the excessiveness of his fury which seized upon him, the ball started out of his head, and some of the brain came after it, and in that way he died. The wood of Lanshraigh, in Feara Rois, is the name by which that shrubby wood is called."

I have imagined Cuchullain meeting Fand "walking among flaming dew". The story of their love is one of the most beautiful of our old tales. Two birds, bound one to another with a chain of gold, came to a lake side where Cuchullain and the host of Uladh was encamped, and sang so sweetly that all the host fell into a magic sleep. Presently they took the shape of two beautiful women, and cast a magical weakness upon Cuchullain, in which he lay for a year. At the year's end an Aengus, who was probably Aengus the master of love, one of the greatest of the children of the goddess Danu, came and sat upon his bedside, and sang how Fand, the wife of Mannannan, the master of the sea, and of the islands of the dead, loved him; and that if he would come into the country of the gods, where there was wine and gold and silver, Fand, and Laban her sister, would heal him of his magical weakness. Cuchullain went to the country of the gods, and, after being for a month the lover of Fand, made her a promise to meet her at a place called "the Yew at the Strand's End", and came back to the earth. Emer, his mortal wife, won his love again, and Mannannan came to "the Yew at the Strand's End", and carried Fand away. When Cuchullain saw her going, his love for her fell upon him again, and he went mad, and wandered among the mountains without food or drink, until he was at last cured by a Druid drink of forgetfulness.

I have founded the man "who drove the gods out of their Liss", or fort, upon something I have read about Caolte after the battle of Gabra, when almost all his companions were killed, driving the gods out of their Liss, either at Osraighe, now Ossory, or at Eas Ruaidh, now Asseroe, a waterfall at Ballyshannon, where Ilbreac, one of the children of the goddess Danu, had a Liss. I am writing away from most of my books, and have not been able to find the passage; but I certainly read it somewhere.

I have founded "the proud dreaming king" upon Fergus, the son of Roigh, the legendary poet of "the quest of the bull of Cualge", as he is in the ancient story of Deirdre, and in modern poems by Ferguson. He married Nessa, and Ferguson makes him tell how she took him "captive in a single look."

> "I am but an empty shade,
> Far from life and passion laid;
> Yet does sweet remembrance thrill
> All my shadowy being still."

Presently, because of his great love, he gave up his throne to Conchobar, her son by another, and lived out his days feasting, and fighting, and hunting. His promise never to refuse a feast from a certain comrade, and the mischief that came by his promise, and the vengeance he took afterwards, are a principal theme of the poets, I have explained my imagination of him in "Fergus and the Druid", and in a little song in the second act of "The Countess Kathleen".

I have founded him "who sold tillage, and house, and goods", upon something in "The Red Pony", a folk tale in Mr. Larminie's "West Irish Folk Tales". A young man "saw a light before him on the high road. When he came as far, there was an open box on the road, and a light coming up out of it. He took up the box. There was a lock of hair in it. Presently he had to go to become the servant of a king for his living. There were eleven boys. When they were going out into the stable at ten o'clock, each of them took a light but he. He took no candle at all with him. Each of them went into his own stable.

When he went into his stable he opened the box. He left it in a hole in the wall. The light was great. It was twice as much as in the other stables." The king hears of it, and makes him show him the box. The king says, "You must go and bring me the woman to whom the hair belongs." In the end, the young man, and not the king, marries the woman.

To a Wealthy Man; September, 1913; To a Friend Whose Work Has Come to Nothing; Paudeen; To a Shade

During the thirty years or so during which I have been reading Irish newspapers, three public controversies have stirred my imagination. The first was the Parnell controversy. There were reasons to justify a man's joining either party, but there were none to justify, on one side or on the other, lying accusations forgetful of past service, a frenzy of detraction. And another was the dispute over "The Playboy". There were reasons for opposing as for supporting that violent, laughing thing, but none for the lies, for the unscrupulous rhetoric spread against it in Ireland, and from Ireland to America. The third prepared for the Corporation's refusal of a building for Sir Hugh Lane's famous collection of pictures.

One could respect the argument that Dublin, with much poverty and many slums, could not afford the £22,000 the building was to cost the city, but not the minds that used it. One frenzied man compared the pictures to Troy horse which "destroyed a city", and innumerable correspondents described Sir Hugh Lane and those who had subscribed many thousands to give Dublin paintings by Corot, Manet, Monet, Degas, and Renoir, as "self-seekers", "self-advertisers", "picture-dealers", "log-rolling cranks and faddists", and one clerical paper told "picture-dealer Lane" to take himself and his pictures out of that. A member of the Corporation said there were Irish artists who could paint as good if they had a mind to, and another described a half-hour in the temporary gallery in Harcourt Street as the most dismal of his life. Some one else asked instead of these eccentric pictures to be given pictures "like those beautiful productions displayed in the windows of our city picture shops." Another thought that we would all be more patriotic if we devoted our energy to fighting the Insurance Act. Another would not hang them in his kitchen, while yet another described the vogue of French impressionist painting as having gone to such a length among "log-rolling enthusiasts" that they even admired "works that were rejected from the Salon forty years ago by the finest critics in the world."

The first serious opposition began in the *Irish Catholic*, the chief Dublin clerical paper, and Mr. William Murphy, the organizer of the recent lock-out and Mr. Healy's financial supporter in his attack upon Parnell, a man of great influence, brought to its support a few days later his newspapers *The Evening Herald* and *The Irish Independent*, the most popular of Irish daily papers. He replied to my poem "To a Wealthy Man" (I was thinking of a very different wealthy man) from what he described as "Paudeen's point of view", and "Paudeen's point of view" it was. The enthusiasm for "Sir Hugh Lane's Corots" – one paper spelled the name repeatedly "Crot" – being but "an exotic fashion", waited "some satirist like Gilbert" who "killed the aesthetic craze", and as for the rest "there were no greater humbugs in the world than art critics and so-called experts." As the first avowed reason for opposition, the necessities of the poor got but a few lines, not so many certainly as the objection of various persons to supply Sir Hugh Lane with "a monument at the city's expense", and as the gallery was supported by Mr.

James Larkin, the chief Labour leader, and important slum workers, I assume that the purpose of the opposition was not exclusively charitable.

These controversies, political, literary, and artistic, have showed that neither religion nor politics can of itself create minds with enough receptivity to become wise, or just and generous enough to make a nation. Other cities have been as stupid – Samuel Butler laughs at shocked Montreal for hiding the Discobolus in a cellar – but Dublin is the capital of a nation, and an ancient race has nowhere else to look for an education. Goethe in *Wilhelm Meister* describes a saintly and naturally gracious woman, who getting into a quarrel over some trumpery detail of religious observance, grows – she and all her little religious community – angry and vindictive. In Ireland I am constantly reminded of that fable of the futility of all discipline that is not of the whole being. Religious Ireland – and the pious Protestants of my childhood were signal examples – thinks of divine things as a round of duties separated from life and not as an element that may be discovered in all circumstance and emotion, while political Ireland sees the good citizen but as a man who holds to certain opinions and not as a man of good will. Against all this we have but a few educated men and the remnants of an old traditional culture among the poor. Both were stronger forty years ago, before the rise of our new middle class which showed as its first public event, during the nine years of the Parnellite split, how base at moments of excitement are minds without culture.

The Dolls

The fable for this poem came into my head while I was giving some lectures in Dublin. I had noticed once again how all thought among us is frozen into "something other than human life". After I had made the poem, I looked up one day into the blue of the sky, and suddenly imagined, as if lost in the blue of the sky, stiff figures in procession. I remembered that they were the habitual image suggested by blue sky, and looking for a second fable called them "The Magi", complimentary forms to those enraged dolls.

Thoughts upon the Present State of the World: Section Six

The country people see at times certain apparitions whom they name now "fallen angels" now "ancient inhabitants of the country", and describe as riding at whiles "with flowers upon the heads of the horses." I have assumed in the sixth poem that these horsemen, now that the times worsen, give way to worse. My last symbol Robert Artisson was an evil spirit much run after in Kilkenny at the start of the fourteenth century. Are not those who travel in the whirling dust also in the Platonic Year?

Leda and the Swan

I wrote 'Leda and the Swan' because the editor of a political review asked me for a poem. I thought, "After the individualist, demagogic movement, founded by Hobbes and popularized by the Encyclopaedists and the French Revolution, we have a soil so exhausted that it cannot grow that crop again for centuries." Then I thought, "Nothing is now possible but some movement from above preceded by some violent annunciation." My fancy began to play with Leda and the Swan for metaphor, and I began this poem, but as I wrote, bird and lady took such possession of the scene that all politics went out of it, and my friend tells me that his "conservative readers would misunderstand the poem."

Meditations in Time of Civil War

These poems were written at Thoor Ballylee in 1922 during the civil war. Before they were finished the Republicans blew up our "ancient bridge" one midnight. They forbade us to leave the house, but were otherwise polite, even saying at last "Goodnight, thank you" as though we had given them the bridge.

Section six: In the West of Ireland we call a starling a stare, and during the civil war one built a hole in the masonry by my bedroom window.

Section seven, stanza II: The cry "Vengeance on the murders of Jacques Molay", Grand Master of the Templars, seems to me fit symbol for those who labour form hatred, and so for sterility in various kinds. It is said to have been incorporated in the ritual of certain Masonic societies of the eighteenth century, and to have fed class-hatred.

Section seven, stanza IV: I have a ring with a hawk and a butterfly upon it, to symbolise the straight road of logic, and so of mechanism, and the crooked road of intuition: "For wisdom is a butterfly and not a gloomy bird of prey."

The Gift of Harun-al-Rashid

This poem is founded on the following passage in a letter of Owen Ahern's, which I am publishing in *A Vision*.

"After the murder for an unknown reason of Jaffer, head of the family of the Barmecides, Harun-al-Rashid seemed as though a great weight had fallen from him, and in the rejoicing of the moment, a rejoicing that seemed to Jaffar's friends a disguise for his remorse, he brought a new bride into the house. Wishing to confer an equal happiness upon his friend, he chose a young bride for Kusta-ben-Luka. According to one tradition of the desert, she had, to the great surprise of her friends, fallen in love with the elderly philosopher, but according to another Harun bought her from a passing merchant. Kusta, a christian like the Caliph's own physician, had planned, one version of the story says, to end his days in a Monastery at Nisibis, while another story has it that he was deep in a violent love affair that he had arranged for himself. The only thing upon which there is general agreement is that he was warned by a dream to accept the gift of the Caliph, and that his wife a few days after the marriage began to talk in her sleep, and that she told him all those things which he had searched for vainly all his life in the great library of the Caliph and in the conversation of wise men. One curious detail has come down to us in Bedouin tradition. When awake she was a merry girl with no more interest in matters of the kind than other girls of her age, and Kusta, the apple of whose eye she had grown to be, fearing that it would make her think his love but self-interest, never told her that she talked to him in her sleep. Michael Robartes frequently heard Bedouins quoting this as proof of Kusta-ben-Luka's extraordinary wisdom… even in the other world Kusta's bride is supposed to remain in ignorance of her share in founding the religion of the Judwalis, and for this reason young girls, who think themselves wise, are ordered by their fathers and mothers to wear little amulets on which her name has been written. All these contradictory stories seem to be a confused recollection of the contents of a little old book, lost many years ago with Kusta-ben-Luka's larger book, in the desert battle which I have already described. This little book was discovered according to tradition, by some Judwali scholar or saint, between the pages of a Greek book which had once been in the Caliph's library. The story of the discovery may however be the invention of a much later age to justify some doctrine, or development of old doctrine, that it may have contained."

In my poem I have greatly elaborated this bare narrative, but I do not think it too great a poetical licence to describe Kusta as hesitating between the poems of Sappho and the treatise of Parmenides as hiding places. Gibbon says the poems of Sappho were still extant in the twelfth century, and it does not seem impossible that a great philosophical work, of which we possess only fragments, may have found its way into an Arab library of the eighth century. Certainly there are passages of Parmenides, that for instance numbered one hundred and thirty by Burkitt, and still more in his immediate predecessors, which Kusta would have recognised as his own thought. This from Herakleitus for instance "Mortals are Immortals and Immortals are Mortals, the one living the other's death and dying the other's life."

Regarding line 7: The banners of the Abbasid Caliphs were black as an act of mourning for those who had fallen in battle at the establishment of the Dynasty.

Towards the end: "All those gyres and cubes and midnight things" refers to the geometrical forms which Robartes describes the Judwali Arabs as making upon the sand for the instruction of their young people, and which, according to tradition, were drawn or described in sleep by the wife of Kusta-ben-Luka.

W.B. YEATS
A Biographical Note

WINNER OF THE NOBEL PRIZE for Literature in 1923, William Butler Yeats (1865–1939) is one of the principal figures in twentieth-century literature, and a distinguished Modernist poet. Despite having spent fourteen years of his childhood in London, Yeats felt a strong affiliation with his home country of Ireland. After attending the Metropolitan School of Art in Dublin, he moved back to London in 1887, where he began life as a professional writer. It was through his involvement in the literary scene there that he encountered Maud Gonne, a rebellious Irish patriot and rhetorician. Her commanding beauty would lead Yeats to join the Irish nationalist cause, and to cast her in the titular role in his 1902 play *Cathleen ni Houlihan*. She would refuse his marriage proposals multiple times, and he would later marry Georgie Hyde-Lees in 1917.

He did not identify strongly with either the Protestant or Catholic faith predominant in Ireland; instead, traditions of Irish folklore and supernatural legend influenced his spiritual philosophy. He endeavoured to create a literature informed by a more ancient and pagan tradition that would transform the country. Yeats' early poetry is notably more dreamlike and colourful in its imagery and use of Irish folklore and legend, but he perfects a more focused style in his later volumes, such as *The Green Helmet* (1910) and *The Tower* (1928). He explores his own philosophy and psychical research in his prose work *The Vision* (first published 1925), reflecting on connections between history, imagination and the occult.

INDEX OF FIRST LINES

INDEX OF POEMS

COLLECTABLE CLASSICS
Complete & Unabridged

The new FLAME TREE COLLECTABLE
CLASSICS are chosen to create a delightful
and timeless home library. Each stunning
edition features deluxe cover treatments,
ribbon markers, luxury endpapers and gilded
edges. The unabridged text is accompanied
by a Glossary of Victorian and Literary Terms
produced for the modern reader.

See our expanding range at
flametreepublishing.com